I0592868

Arcane
Awakenings
Books Three and Four

SHELLEY RUSSELL NOLAN

Creator: Nolan, Shelley Russell, author.
Title: Arcane Awakenings Books Three and Four / Shelley Russell Nolan
ISBN: 978-0-6481683-2-4

Subjects: Fantasy fiction

Printed in Australia by Ingram Spark
Cover design: Mariah Sinclair

www.shelleyrussellnolan.com

Also by Shelley Russell Nolan

The Reaper Series

Lost Reaper
Winged Reaper
Silver Reaper

Arcane Awakenings Series

Arcane Awakenings Books One and Two

For Jennifer

Contents

Book One

Hidden Aftershock

1

The dream wrapped around me, an intoxicating blend of fear and wonder, drawing me deeper and deeper.

I was back at the Wood Estate, standing in the hallway leading to the room I'd been confined to after my last escape failed. The floor undulated beneath me, making it hard to maintain my footing. Cracks appeared in the walls as the earthquake built in intensity, parts of the ceiling collapsing to the floor.

I ignored the chaos, my focus fixed on my old room.

The door was ajar enough to let a narrow beam of light spill into the hallway. Unbridled power swirled within the room, accompanied by a scent reminding me of lush green grass and rich soil, inviting and sweet. The sheer magnitude of the power washed over me in a wave that set my pulse racing. I'd never got this close before, most of the dreams cutting off once I'd exited the stairwell and spotted my room at the end of the hall. This time it felt different; the very air around me charged with possibility.

Three steps.

That was all it would take for me to see who waited inside.

I took the first step.

Then another.

My sleeping body jolted, the movement tipping me out of the dream.

'No!' My shout sounded only in my head as I bolted upright, fists clenching the sheets. I sagged against the bedhead, groaning as the remnants of the dream danced around me, tantalising me with what might have been.

I'd come so close.

My eyes struggled to adjust to the dark of night, thick curtains blocking the light from the lamppost outside my bedroom window. The thrill of power unleashed somewhere nearby thrummed through my body, making me gasp. It hadn't been a dream. The earthquake was real, a deep rumble sounding a split second before the house shook around me.

I let instinct take over, sending my mind soaring, already sure of what I would find.

Sure enough, just like the other times I'd done this, my mental probe travelled west, out of Easton, in the direction of the estate. The power surging in the air around me was raw, uncontained, giving off that rich earthy scent.

The power felt undeniably male.

I focused on the feel of it, wrapping my consciousness round it and sending out my own power in a calm wave. Tears pricked my eyes at the emotional turmoil flooding through the tenuous connection I'd made. The turmoil came because of burgeoning powers in someone with no idea what they were or how to control them.

I tried to connect on a deeper level with the person who had created the earthquake, to let them know they weren't alone and that I was there to help them. But the distance was too great, diluting the strength of my sending. My head spun as I did my best to reach them. A flare of surprise travelled back along the line of power feeding the earthquake. It wavered for a moment before pushing me away, casting my mental probe adrift somewhere between home and the estate.

A car alarm shrieked nearby, pulling me back to myself.

I drew my knees to my chest, wrapping my arms around them as the bed continued to shake, books falling from the shelves above the desk on the far wall. I stretched out an arm to secure the lamp on my bedside table before it could topple to the floor.

Faint cries filled the night as our neighbours woke to find themselves amidst yet another earthquake. The shaking continued for what seemed like hours, but would have been less than a minute.

A shadowed figure appeared in the open doorway to my room moments after the last of the shaking subsided.

'Angel, are you okay?' Daniel reached out and switched on the light.

Blinking against the sudden brightness, I unwound my limbs and brushed hair out of my eyes as I gave him a nod.

'That one lasted twice as long as any of the other quakes. Felt stronger too,' said Andie, appearing in the doorway behind him. She nudged Daniel aside and came to sit on my bed, dark blonde hair identical to mine falling in loose tangles over her shoulders.

'They're only going to get worse,' I told her through the telepathic bond we shared. 'He's getting stronger, with little to no control of his abilities.'

Tonight had been the closest I'd come to connecting with him, before I'd been pushed away.

Andie grimaced. 'More earthquakes. Something to look forward to. Not.'

Celeste poked her head into the room, flame-coloured hair tamed by a braid. 'Are you sure someone like us is behind the earthquakes, Angel? I still don't sense anything.'

'Hey,' said Daniel, before I could answer her. 'You guys aren't supposed to have conversations where I can't join in. I've been working hard on my signing. It's not fair if you girls won't let me use it.'

My smile was rueful as I made the sign for "sorry". He

5

was right. He had been working hard, him and Nick, at the sign language classes the three of us went to on a Tuesday and Thursday evening at the Easton Community Centre. I loved knowing both he and Andie's boyfriend were determined to be able to communicate with me, without my having to write everything down on a whiteboard as Dr Wood had forced me to do.

So far, Celeste and Andie were the only people who could hear my mental voice. Celeste was like me, possessing psychic abilities, while Andie was a reservoir of power I could tap into as her identical twin. I frowned, thinking about the earthquake. Perhaps the guy who had created it would be able to hear me as well.

But first I had to find him.

I faced my family, and focused on making the correct signs so Daniel could follow along with what I was broadcasting to Andie and Celeste.

'I'm sure. His pain and confusion fill the air each time a quake hits.'

Andie narrowed her eyes. 'You still think it's the missing patient, the one Celeste knocked out?'

Celeste's cheeks paled, making the fine dusting of freckles across her nose stand out even more.

'It's the only explanation that makes sense,' I signed for Daniel's benefit, though Andie and Celeste would hear my words in their head. 'Celeste said energy flared between them when he touched her. I think that first moment of contact must have sparked his latent ability.'

'We don't know for sure it was their first contact,' said Andie. 'She could have been touched by the guy a thousand times while she was catatonic. Or even before that. With Celeste having no memory of her life prior to when she woke up at the estate, we have no way of knowing for sure.'

Celeste flushed. 'I may not have my memory back, but I'm pretty sure I'm not the type of girl to go around touching strange guys. Besides, Dr Wood kept me locked away to make sure I didn't contaminate her research data. I think I was only stuck in general population once she'd fried my brain.'

Daniel reached out and wrapped Celeste in his arms. 'Andie didn't mean it like that.'

'I know. It's fine. I'm just saying, Angel could be right. The same kind of energy was present the first time I touched Angel, only it was gentler. What if that was because both of us already had our abilities awakened? Call me crazy, but it makes me wonder if the same thing would happen any time either of us encountered someone who also had powers, latent or otherwise.'

Andie snorted. 'I can just imagine how well that would go down. The two of you could go to shake someone's hand and wind up knocking them unconscious. Maybe both of you should invest in a thick pair of gloves.'

'I'm sure we'll be fine,' I said, and signed. 'We'll just have to be careful to keep contact with strangers to a minimum. We have more important stuff to worry about right now. If it is Ethan Rhodes causing the earthquakes, you can bet Dr Wood is behind it.'

Andie gave a shudder. 'And isn't that an unpleasant thought.'

'There's been no sign of her, or the hulk of an orderly who worked for her, since their slimy lawyer got them released on a technicality,' said Daniel.

Dr Wood and Karl Sypher had disappeared before the police could get their case in order and return to the estate to arrest them for a second time.

'Do you really think she'd be stupid enough to come back to Easton, knowing they're on the look-out for her?' Daniel asked.

'Yes,' Andie and Celeste said at the same time as I signed it.

'She's obsessed with her research, and proving the scientists who ridiculed her all those years ago were wrong,' I added.

No one said anything for a long moment, and I was sure they were all thinking the same thing. They'd thought we were free, safe. It was a sobering thought to realise the life we'd built for our little family over the last couple of months could be taken away from us at any moment.

We'd moved into the sprawling four-bedroom house one month ago, after Celeste received the remaining money left in the trust fund her father had set up for her. The fund lawyers had also arranged the sale of the estate. Around the same time, after numerous sessions with doctors, psychologists and counsellors, I'd finally been approved for a government allowance, which enabled me to cover my share of the rent for a bigger place.

Nick had helped with the move, and I'd covered my bedroom walls with photos of the five of us. After six months of having to stare at the blank and impersonal walls of the room that had been my cell, only allowed out at night for exercise, I'd been determined to fill this one with colour and treasured memories. The knowledge Dr Wood was out there, biding her time, planning how to take this away from me, made it all the more precious. I would not let her ruin the new life I'd created, or the family I loved. But I also couldn't forget the rest of her victims.

'We have to find Ethan. Help him.' A strange feeling of peace settled over me after I said it. This was the right thing to do.

'Hang on a minute. How are we supposed to help the guy

when we don't know where he is, or even if he's in trouble?'

I lifted my chin and looked at Daniel. 'I know exactly where he is.'

'The Wood Estate,' said Celeste. 'That's where you said the power surges are coming from. That's where you think he is, right?' Her voice rose. 'You want us to go back there.'

I sent a wave of reassurance toward her. 'You don't need to come. I can go on my own.'

'Like hell you will,' said Daniel.

'You're not going anywhere near that place without me,' said Andie. 'And anyway, it was sold. Surely the new owners would've noticed if a guy who can create earthquakes with his mind was running through the halls?'

Celeste shook her head. 'The lawyer for the trust fund said the new owners can't move in until the police have completed their investigation. At our last meeting he said that was a month away, at least.'

'Fine,' said Andie, arms crossed in front of her chest. 'The place should still be empty, but what if it's not? What if the earthquakes, Angel's dreams, all of it, is a way for Dr Wood to lure us back there?'

Andie was right. This could be a trap, but it didn't matter either way. 'If Ethan doesn't get help soon his powers will continue to spiral out of control. He could easily reduce Easton to rubble. We can't let that happen.'

Celeste lifted her chin, a determined set to her features. 'If you say Ethan needs our help, then I'm coming too. Besides, the three of us proved more than a match for Dr Wood last time.'

'The police have checked every inch of the estate,' said Daniel, staring over at me. 'There was no sign of Dr Wood, this Ethan guy, or the orderly. What makes you think we'll have more luck when all you're basing your theory on is a feeling? Celeste has the same kind of powers as you, but she's not getting the same impression.'

Celeste twisted in Daniel's arms and gazed up at him. 'I've had my powers for a few months. Angel's had hers since she was born. If she says whoever is causing the earthquakes is at the estate, then that's good enough for me.'

'I'm not saying I don't believe her. I'm just saying we need to be smart about this. We can't race off to the estate in the middle of the night.' He looked over at me. 'If we're doing this, we do it properly. Nick and I have a rostered day off tomorrow. Andie can call Nick, and then the five of us will go out there together. When it comes to the estate, and Celeste's crazy mother, there's no way the three of you are going there without us.'

Celeste grimaced at the mention of her mother, but made no protest as Daniel ushered her and Andie back to bed. There were still a few hours before daylight, but even though I lay back down I knew I wouldn't be able to sleep.

Come morning, I would finally get to follow the power behind the earthquakes back to the source.

Ethan Rhodes.

I'd seen his picture in a police report, when I'd been at the station to make a statement. The officer in charge of the investigation into Dr Wood's illegal activities had shown me his photo, asking if I recognised him.

I'd stared at the image of a smiling and confident young man with messy black hair and laughing green eyes, unable to understand how someone like him had found himself at an institution that treated mentally ill youth. Then again, I was aware outward appearances could hide a lifetime of pain and suffering.

I'd never met him before, but as I'd gazed at his picture I'd felt a connection, a ripple of awareness that made me think

I did know him in some way. It wasn't until the next earthquake, a week later, that I realised what the connection was.

He was the source of the power surge the day Andie, Celeste and I had confronted Dr Wood at the estate. More importantly, it was Ethan I'd sensed the night before that, when we'd fled with the proof we needed to have Dr Wood arrested. Something had called to me from the lowest level, making me hesitate as we'd made our escape.

I'd felt his confusion and pain, no doubt caused by having his latent powers awakened after he'd encountered Celeste; powers that had resulted in him being locked away by Dr Wood, to be experimented on, tortured, as I'd been.

He'd needed my help, called out for it, and I'd let myself be pulled away, leaving him trapped and alone.

I'd failed him.

I would not fail him again.

Tomorrow we would return to the estate and I would free Ethan Rhodes.

2

A curious mix of dread and excitement weighed heavily in the pit of my stomach as I looked at the wrought iron gates barring access to the Wood Estate. A large padlock secured the chain holding the gates closed.

I'd wanted this, was sure the dreams, the earthquakes, everything, had been leading me to this point, yet I hesitated to take the next step. Ethan might need my help, but that didn't mean he would welcome my arrival in his life.

Still, staring at the gate wasn't going to help anyone.

I walked up to it, conscious of my family and friends at my back, and tested the give in the chain. There was just enough slack to push the two halves of the gate apart to allow a small person to squeeze between them. Andie, Celeste and I would be able to fit through without any problem, but it would be a tight squeeze for Daniel and Nick.

'Want me to grab the bolt cutters out of the boot?' Nick asked.

Daniel moved to stand beside his friend, brow creased. 'Don't think the police would appreciate us damaging their property.' He pointed to the crime scene tape looped through the fence itself.

'Okay then, on to Plan B.' Nick returned to his car and parked it as close as possible to the wide brick column from which the right side of the gate hung. He and Daniel climbed on top of the car and shimmied over the wall. Once on the other side, they held the gate as far open as the chain would allow so Andie, Celeste and I could slip through the gap without scraping half our skin off in the process.

None of us spoke as we began the trek down the long winding driveway to the main building. The only sounds came from the crunch of our feet on the bitumen, and the soft chirps of birds nesting in the many trees lining the driveway.

Despite the seemingly idyllic setting, shadows cast by those trees set a shiver racing over my body. I looked at the spot where Andie, Celeste and I made our stand three months earlier. The grass had grown wild, leaving no trace of the tumultuous events that had taken place. It felt almost surreal, like walking through an enchanted forest, one hiding a multitude of dangers to trap the unwary.

The closer we got, the harder it became to breathe. Celeste and Andie took my hands, and I didn't need to look at them to know they were as anxious as me. But none of our steps faltered.

Hand in hand, with Daniel and Nick at our backs, we marched on to confront our memories.

I wasn't sure who this was harder for, them or me. Celeste had to be thinking about her mother, not that she ever referred to Dr Wood as such. Andie's thoughts were sure to be filled with regret. It still pained her to think she'd forgotten my existence. No matter how many times I told her it wasn't her fault, that she'd had nothing to do with it, she still felt guilty because I'd been locked away for so long.

Daniel also carried a burden of guilt. He'd believed his adoptive parents when they told him I'd died in the fire that killed our mother and father. He'd accepted their reasoning for not telling Andie she'd had an identical twin. To find out fifteen years later he'd been lied to, and to then witness what I'd endured at the estate, made him even more protective now. And not just of me. His innate sense of responsibility had increased tenfold when it came to Andie and Celeste. For him to agree to come here at all was a huge sign of his faith in the three of us and our ability to handle any situation.

As we rounded the last curve in the driveway I caught my first glimpse of the squat grey building with bars on the windows of the top two floors, and a lump appeared in my throat. I hoped Daniel's faith in me was justified. I had to find Ethan, and help him control his power before one of his earthquakes tore Easton apart.

With a tight grip on Andie's and Celeste's hands, I approached the double doors in the centre of the ground floor.

Police tape stretched across the glass, flapping in a slight breeze.

The tape had loosened from months of exposure to the weather, but was still intact. The front doors hadn't been opened since the police finished their last search for evidence. They'd kept us informed during the initial stages of the investigation, but contact had been limited since then. The young police officer who watched the recording of Celeste being tortured by her mother was the only one who kept in touch with us. Dr Wood's orderlies had drugged him when he and his partner tried to stop them taking Celeste, Andie and me back to the estate, and I guess he felt responsible for us.

It was Constable Scott Carlton who let us know Dr Wood had taken the rest of the tapes with her when she disappeared. The last time he contacted us was with unwelcome information. Her lawyer had successfully petitioned the Justice Department to have the tapes Daniel and Nick handed to the police destroyed due to the same technicality that saw Dr Wood released.

While on one level I was glad to know the tapes, which showed years of testing of my abilities were less likely to be made public, the thought of Dr Wood's motive for taking them was a cause for concern. The sole reason for her filming the sessions was to prove her theories were correct. It was only a matter of time before she decided to go public with what she'd discovered, and when she did all chance of a normal life would be lost to us.

But that was a problem for another time.

Eyes closed, I tuned out my inner turmoil and focused on the sensations coming to me from within the building itself. With the extra boost from the reservoir of power Andie contained, I was able to probe further, deeper, searching for any sign of Ethan. I found no hint of him; the rich earthiness I associated with his power absent from the space around me.

I had no trouble picking out the flashes of silver that signified Celeste's ability to create lightning and manipulate electrical currents, or the shimmering well of energy contained in Andie's core. Daniel and Nick, though they held no psychic ability, were also easy to detect, their physical presence registering as a flickering flame, so it couldn't be a failure of my abilities to detect another presence.

Either Ethan had found a way to hide his presence or we were the only people at the estate.

Even more frustrating was the lack of what Dr Wood had termed my precognitive sense, where I would see what was going to happen before an event occurred. I could predict what card would be turned up next with relative ease, and choose a route to take to avoid trouble for others with a fair amount of certainty if I concentrated and was well rested. Yet I'd been unable to see anything about Ethan, or the whereabouts and plans of Dr Wood.

I opened my eyes and faced the others. 'I'm not picking up anybody nearby. We should split up. Andie and Nick, can you check down the right side of the building? The rest of us will take the left.'

Andie and I would be able to communicate despite the

separation, to let the other team know if we found anything. Celeste would be able to translate my words for Daniel if I had no time to concentrate on using sign language.

It was slow going as we headed toward the back of the building. The police had cut open a section of the electric fence that blocked off the back of the estate, but we had to navigate our way through a jungle of overgrown bushes and long grass. I was pleased I'd had the foresight to wear jeans as we fought our way to the side of the building to peer through the barred windows on ground level.

After the tenth time we stopped to untangle ourselves, I let Andie know we were heading straight for the back entrance. Each glimpse through the windows had shown the same thing, furniture upturned in otherwise empty rooms. I didn't think any of the other windows would provide us with anything different to look at.

Andie and Nick were waiting at the back door when we rounded the corner of the building. I already knew they hadn't found anything of significance, so didn't hesitate to place my hand on the door handle and give it a twist.

It failed to turn, which was to be expected. But this door was missing the crime scene tape. Was this because the police had forgotten it, or had it been removed after their last official visit? I scanned the flower beds on either side of the doorway. There was no sign of it, but it could have easily been carried away and discarded elsewhere if someone had used this door to enter the building recently.

I cast out my senses to search for anyone who might be nearby.

I didn't find anyone, but a weird shiver swept over my body. It felt as though eyes were on me, boring into the back of my head. I twisted and cast my senses out into the unkempt garden that had once been the haven for patients when they were allowed outside for exercise. I was only allowed in the garden at night, with two orderlies watching my every move, after a succession of failed escape attempts.

I found nothing, and reached out to take Andie's hand to push my senses further.

The impression of someone watching me remained, the slight shiver spreading to envelop my entire body, but all with no sign or sense of who they were.

'Is everything okay? Is someone out there?' Celeste moved to take my other hand, and I got the sense of her casting out her own net. I could tell by the shape of her energy flow she had come up as empty as me. If someone was out there, they were able to shield themselves from us.

I turned my back on whoever was watching me and threaded a loop of power into the lock mechanism, twisting the handle and opening the door.

Beside me, Celeste took a deep breath before being the first to step back into the estate. The rest of us crowded in after her, and I made sure to close and lock the door once we were all inside. The thought of leaving it open, at our backs, with an unknown observer out there, did not sit well with me even though I was usually the first to want a door left open.

This was a consequence of being locked up for most of my life.

None of us spoke as we moved through the ground level, travelling as a group. It appeared the others were just as wary of separating as I was while we systemically checked each room we came across.

The estate appeared to have weathered the recent run of earthquakes with minimal damage, small cracks appearing in some of the walls, but nothing suggesting the foundations or overall structure had been affected. The items left behind had not been so lucky.

The doors to the storerooms either side of the hall were open, allowing us to see the chaos within. Boxes were strewn all over the floor, their contents left to spill out. It was the same level of chaos when I reached the common room, chairs and tables upturned, the televisions fixed to the walls with screens smashed, games and books once enjoyed by the patients scattered everywhere.

'This was not caused by an earthquake,' said Nick as he surveyed the wanton destruction, 'and there is no way the police would have done it.'

'Do you think squatters have been staying here?' Daniel asked.

Squatters. My pulse quickened. What if they were still inside? I cast out my senses once again, but still found no sign of any occupants, squatter or otherwise.

'Could have been vandals I guess,' said Andie, skirting a broken table.

'Long way out of town to come just to break stuff,' said Celeste.

'It was all over the news after this place was shut down. Any number of people could have come out here once the police had done their bit,' said Daniel.

'Or the new owners might have decided not to wait to lay claim to the place, and had a little fun throwing things around,' said Nick with a shrug.

I didn't care about who else might have been here, vandals or otherwise. I was here for Ethan. I left the common room behind, the others following in my wake, making for the alcove that housed the elevator and the stairwell.

The display above the elevator was blank. Nick flicked a light switch to confirm the electricity had been cut to the entire building.

'Good thing we brought torches,' he said with a grin as he

pulled one from his back pocket and switched it on.

Daniel did the same as the five of us neared the exit door for the stairwell. Unlike every other door in the place, this one was locked. With no electricity to work the keypad, the door handle didn't budge when I checked it.

'Here, let me,' said Celeste, her voice barely above a whisper as she placed her hand on the keypad.

A soft crackle sounded, and a spark flashed as she sent a tiny bolt of electricity into the unit. The display lit up and the handle moved easily when I tried again. We filed through the doorway, Daniel using the remains of a chair from the common room to prop it open before we started the slow trek down the stairs to the third basement level, torches filling the stairwell with shadows.

This was where my dreams had taken me every night.

Here, I would find out once and for all if there really was something or someone waiting for me.

3

I held my breath as I stepped out of the stairwell on the last level and slowly approached my old room. Memories of the time I'd spent here threatened to overwhelm me and I pushed them aside, wiping sweaty palms on the legs of my jeans. This was not about me. This was about finding Ethan, helping him come to terms with his newfound abilities and teaching him how to control and harness them.

My pulse pounded in my ears when I got close enough to see the door was slightly ajar, just like in my dreams, although there was no light shining out from within. I wasn't alone, and we weren't in the midst of an earthquake, but the similarities still had me breathing fast as I reached out to push the door open.

Tears pricked my eyes at what I found.

An empty room, bed unmade, the chain that had once encircled my ankle still dangling from a hook embedded deep into the wall above it.

It wasn't seeing my old room, or the chain used to bind me, that caused my tears. I'd been so sure, despite everything that told me the place was deserted, that I would find Ethan here. It felt as if I'd been robbed of something precious.

I forced a smile and turned to face the others. 'There's nothing here,' I said, hoping my mental voice gave no hint of the dismay bubbling away inside me.

When Andie and Celeste moved to comfort me, I knew I'd failed.

Even Nick and Daniel were sending me sympathetic looks

as we shuffled back toward the stairwell.

'Do you think it's worth checking the other floors? Seeing if there is anything we might have missed?' said Daniel.

I shook my head. 'If anyone was here, they're long gone.'

'Someone is creating the earthquakes,' said Celeste. 'Angel can sense their power, and their lack of control over it. We need to find them.'

'Honestly, I'm not sure what I'm sensing. Maybe the experts are right, and the earthquakes are caused by a fault line so deep their instruments can't detect it.' I worked hard to not show what I truly thought about the so-called experts and their opinions.

Andie gave a snort. 'Those idiots have no clue what's causing the earthquakes. They come up with a different theory after each one, all to cover their own butts for not being able to provide concrete answers. Your theory makes much more sense.'

'Andie's right,' said Nick. 'It has to be someone like Angel and Celeste behind the earthquakes, not an undiscovered fault line. Not to mention they have only been happening since you all escaped from this place. We just came here at the wrong time. Either that or this Rhodes guy is a champion at hide and seek.'

I let their support and confidence in my abilities buoy me up as we returned to the ground floor and made our way to the back door. As soon as I was out in the open, the sensation of eyes on me returned.

With the niggle of being under observation occupying my thoughts, it wasn't until we reached the gate that the problem of how to get Nick and Daniel over the fence hit me. There were no conveniently placed trees to help them scale the three-metre fence, and Nick had left his set of bolt cutters in the boot of his car.

In the end it was a matter of having Nick provide the boost for Daniel to scramble over the fence. I then used my powers to create a stable, and invisible, platform for Nick to use to gain the extra height needed to enable him to climb over. The dubious look on his face as he put his trust in something he couldn't see made us all laugh.

I was in a much better frame of mind as Andie, Celeste and I slipped through the gap between the gates and made our way to the car. All I had to worry about next was convincing them I didn't need a babysitter for my counselling session at the Community Centre that afternoon.

It took a while, but I finally managed to get them to let me have this moment of independence, though I was sure they only said yes to stop me dwelling on not being able to find Ethan. Maybe Nick was right, and he had somehow managed to hide himself from me.

If Ethan was in hiding, all I could do was continue to reach out to him when his powers surged and hope next time he would accept my offer of help. For now, I would enjoy the simple pleasure of being without a chaperone for an afternoon.

My sense of pleasure quickly fled when a rumble announced the arrival of yet another earthquake minutes into my session with Dr O'Hanlon. This was followed moments later by the shifting of the floor beneath the couch I sat on.

I tensed, counting each second the earthquake lasted, ignoring the bangs as books fell off the shelves lining one wall of the counsellor's office.

One minute and forty-seven seconds.

This had been the longest quake so far, and the feeling of unbridled power flowing along with it was also stronger, setting a wave of shivers over my body. It was so raw, elemental, my heart pounded as I sifted through the sensations singing in the air around me. There was no mistaking the earthy overtones I'd come to associate with the person responsible for the quakes. But this was the first time there had been two less than a day apart. It couldn't be a coincidence, this one occurring so soon after I'd been out to the estate.

Someone had been watching me.

Was it Ethan?

If so, how had he masked himself from me?

As I had the night before, I tried to follow the power surge back to the source, but it ebbed away before I could pin it down. There was just enough time for me to get a vague sense of the direction it came from, west, toward the estate.

I nibbled my bottom lip. It had to be Ethan.

'Angel. It's okay. You're safe here.'

I released my lip and managed a smile for Dr O'Hanlon as she scooped up the fallen books and replaced them on the shelves, stifling a sigh at her well-intentioned comments. She had no way of knowing my concern was not for the quake itself, but from where it originated.

How could she know?

It wasn't as though I could tell her.

Coming clean would inevitably wind up with me being sent to another institution; one I might never escape from if the truth about me were to be known.

I rubbed my right ankle, smoothing my fingers over the raised scar from almost six months of being chained to a wall as punishment for attempting to escape.

I would never be chained again.

'Are you still dreaming about earthquakes?' Dr O'Hanlon asked, bringing my thoughts back to the here and now as she resumed her seat on the chair opposite the couch.

I shrugged, and made the sign for sometimes.

That was a lie, of course. But there was no need for her to know how often I'd had the dream. As the quakes in the real world strengthened, along with my awareness of the person behind them, so too did the frequency of the dream and its hold on me.

Each time I exited the stairwell, and made my way to the start of the hall, something would always jar me from my sleep. I'd come back to myself, fists clenched as I was once again cheated out of discovering who was drawing me back there, increasingly convinced it was Ethan Rhodes.

I'd experienced the feeling for real that afternoon.

'It's understandable for you to associate the earthquakes with your time at the Wood Estate. The quakes started shortly after your siblings rescued you. Your subconscious sees them as a symbol of the upheaval in your life. The dreams should stop once you have fully come to terms with your new life and your place in it.' Dr O'Hanlon gave me a kindly smile.

'You were locked away from the world, and your loved ones, for fifteen years. I know all you wanted was to be reunited with them, but reality rarely matches our dreams. It will take time to process all the changes that come with being released. You have the language barrier to overcome, as well as the added pressure to fill the gaps in your formal education. With so much going on in your life, the stimuli can be overwhelming at times.'

I worked to make my grimace look more like a smile. I'd received basic schooling while at the estate, sitting in on lessons with the other patients, but had no accreditation to show what I'd learned. The online course I was currently enrolled in to allow me to obtain a Certificate of Education, the equivalent of completing high school, was actually enjoyable. The only pressure I felt was to keep up with Celeste, who was also taking the course to make up for her memory loss. The two of us had made a game of it, challenging each other to finish each module with top marks.

No, it wasn't the language barrier or my continuing education that caused my sleepless nights. The earthquakes were solely to blame for that. Fear for what would happen when the situation escalated, as was inevitable, kept me distracted for the rest of the hour-long session. I signed when appropriate, only half listening to Dr O'Hanlon. Finally, she wrapped up the session and stood to see me out.

It was hard to contain my relief as I signed a farewell and headed for the door, nodding fervently at her reminder to confirm my next counselling session in a week's time. I dutifully made my way to the reception area and waited with concealed impatience as the permanently cheerful receptionist completed the paperwork for today's session and made sure everything was ready for the next one.

'Is Daniel picking you up today?' Her smile was hopeful.

I'd caught her casting admiring looks Daniel's way on many occasions, and she wasn't the only one I'd noticed checking out my handsome brother or Nick when they joined me for sign language classes. I shook my head and made the signs to indicate he was taking Celeste for a driving lesson. Her smile dimmed at the reminder Daniel had a girlfriend, but she soon rallied.

'Would you like me to call you a taxi?'

I shook my head and held up the mobile phone Daniel had purchased for me several weeks ago, showing her the app on the home screen that enabled me to order a taxi without needing to speak. She handed me an appointment card with the time and date for my next session neatly handwritten on the back.

I tucked the card into my back pocket, waved goodbye, and moved to the front doors. The centre had seats out the front, in a spacious shaded area, and I sat down and opened the app to request a taxi.

After I filled out the section for my pick-up location, the screen flicked to the section for where I wanted to go. My home address was the only one programmed in so far, but I paused before hitting the submit button.

Daniel had packed a picnic lunch for him and Celeste to enjoy after the driving lesson he'd promised her the week before, and Andie and Nick were at the movies, meaning I'd be returning to an empty house. Not that I minded being alone, but this was the first time since I'd escaped the estate I didn't have either of my siblings hovering over me.

I lifted my head, seeing but not really taking any notice of the people coming and going from the centre. In every single one of my dreams about the estate I'd been alone. What if I hadn't found anything, or anyone, there today because the others had been with me?

Would the mysterious observer have made themselves visible if I'd been alone?

I typed the address for the estate into the taxi app, submitting the request before I could change my mind. Then I put the phone away, hands clasped tightly in front of me as I waited for the taxi to arrive.

My phone buzzed seconds later, startling a silent gasp from me. I pulled it out of my pocket and checked the screen.

It was a text from Daniel.

Hope appt with doc good. Celeste did great with lesson. Heading 2 park 4 lunch. Want us 2 pick you up?

I quickly typed back a reply, urging them to go and enjoy their picnic, for once glad to be mute. If he had been able to call me, and hear my voice, there was no way I would have been able to talk normally enough to not make him suspicious.

Once I hit send, I worked to calm my nerves, worried Andie would be able to sense the rising mix of excitement and dread I felt at the thought of returning to the estate on my own. I hoped she was too caught up in spending time with Nick and the movie to spare a thought for me. The bond that allowed us to communicate telepathically was always stronger when we were together, but extreme emotions often travelled long distances. I would have to be careful there was no leakage, at least until I'd been to the estate and uncovered the truth once and for all.

The taxi finally pulled up at the kerb out front of the centre. I hurried over to it and climbed inside, smiling at the driver as he greeted me. He had clearly picked up patrons of the centre before as I didn't have to work hard to get him to understand my silent explanation to show I couldn't talk. Then I held up my phone to show him the taxi app and he gave me a nod and thumbs up.

He showed no hesitation in filling the silence as he pulled out into traffic, and I let his words wash over me as a distraction from what I was about to do, and the eventual fallout once the others found out. There would be no way I could keep it hidden from Andie or Celeste when we were face to face. I'd be forced to come clean, and I winced anticipating their reaction. I just hoped they'd understand why I had to do this, for my sanity if for no other reason.

I'd been able to hide the worst of the toll the dreams were taking on me, but I couldn't keep it up indefinitely, and neither could Ethan.

Despite my conviction I was doing the right thing, it was hard to sit still, to not fidget as the taxi drew closer to the estate. I had few pleasant memories of my time here. This morning I'd gone in with Andie and Celeste at my side, confident of our combined ability to take on any threat. Now it was just me. The memory of how helpless I'd been for so long had me fearing I would not have what it took to protect myself if I was confronted with danger.

The taxi driver must have sensed my unease as his endless chatter petered off into silence. My eyes were fixed on the road ahead of us, muscles tensing when the large double gates came into view. The taxi rolled to a stop in front of them, and the driver twisted around to look at me, concern in his eyes.

'Are you sure about this, miss? Doesn't look like they're expecting visitors.'

My cheeks ached with the effort to show him an untroubled smile. I nodded enthusiastically, eyes wide, unbuckled my seatbelt, and handed him the card to pay for the fare.

I hoped I wasn't making a huge mistake.

4

I marched up to the gates and slipped through the gap between the two sides, all without taking a breath.

On the other side, I spared a moment to wave goodbye to the taxi driver, who still hadn't left. Then, with shoulders back and head held high, I walked down the driveway for the second time that day. I didn't slow my pace until I heard the taxi pull away.

I let out the breath I'd been holding, and some of the tension gripping my body was expelled along with it. I'd been sure this visit would end just as frustratingly empty as the last one if the taxi driver hadn't left. I was sure I had to be alone to uncover the secret hidden at the heart of the estate. Heartbeat thudding throughout my body, I worked to banish the fears that had overwhelmed me during the journey.

A whisper on the wind, sighed through the trees lining the driveway, brought me to a halt, sure someone had called my name. I felt eyes on me but saw no one, and sensed nothing, just like this morning. I spun in a slow circle, hearing my name once again but unable to find the source of the whisper.

I ran my teeth over my bottom lip, looking back toward the front gates. I put a hand in my back pocket and touched my phone. Perhaps I'd been too hasty in sending the taxi driver away. Dr O'Hanlon's comment about reality rarely matching the dream swam through my mind. What if Andie was right and my dreams about the earthquakes and coming to the estate were a trap devised by Dr Wood?

No. That was crazy.

Dr Wood had been testing for psychic abilities, but she had never displayed any herself. To send me the dreams, to cause the earthquakes, that would take someone with power. And she'd been right in front of me when the first earthquake occurred. I knew the shape and scent of her mind intimately, and there had never been a hint of earthiness. Hers had been a caustic mix of ambition and hate, a volatile combination that coloured every action she made. I didn't need psychic ability to know she was the type of person to poison those around her.

It couldn't be her.

Could it?

Standing in the middle of the driveway worrying over it was getting me no closer to finding answers. I released my grip on the phone and squared my shoulders yet again, determined not to let fear stop me from uncovering the truth. I started walking toward the main building, the sensation of eyes on me growing stronger with every step. But I did not, would not, falter.

The only thing I was sure of was that someone was reaching out to me, desperate to get my attention, and it was time for me to find out who it was.

I edged around the side of the building, slipping through the gap in the electric fence and making for the back entrance we had used that morning. The sensation of being watched had faded, but I reached for the well of power that existed deep within my body. Heat tingled in my fingertips as I prepared to defend myself with fire.

If this did turn out to be a trap, I would not let Dr Wood take me.

Power thrumming through every inch of me, I navigated around the overgrown flower beds and made my way toward the back door. Once I reached it I sucked in a deep breath before testing the handle.

It gave easily.

I froze.

Had we left it unlocked that morning, or had someone else been there since?

I thought back, straining to remember if any of us had locked the door. I'd made a point to do so after we'd first entered the building, but knew I hadn't done the same as we exited, and could not remember one of the others doing it either.

I cast out my senses, again searching for any sign I was not alone. And once again I came up empty. Flashes of life flared far in the distance, in both directions of the estate, possibly occupants of vehicles travelling along the highway, but as far as I could tell I was the only human being on the grounds itself.

I swallowed heavily and pushed the door open, careful not to let it bang into the wall. If there was someone inside the building who had escaped detection, I didn't want to alert them to my presence by making a loud entrance.

I scanned the hallway that led to the common room.

This was it.

I was finally going to discover what it was about this place that haunted me.

Only, this was nothing like my dream.

Instead of a violent earthquake, the reality was grimly silent and still. It felt as if I was the last person on Earth, as if all noise would be deadened before it could even begin. I wiped my hands on my jeans one more time and stepped inside.

Once again, I cast out my senses, searching for the spark of another person. My frown deepened when my probing met a blank wall and rebounded, causing an ache behind my eyes.

That had never happened to me before.

I rubbed my temples, cautiously feeling for the wall.

There.

A dense pocket of resistance existed within the large dining and kitchen area that had been utilised by both patients and staff.

I walked slowly toward the corridor that led to the dining room, stepping lightly between the debris in my path. When I reached the open doorway, I took a deep breath before peeking inside.

The lights weren't on, but the large windows running the length of the room gave me enough light to see by. This room, like the common room, had been ransacked; tables and chairs broken and scattered. All except for one table pressed against the far wall, and the chair neatly placed beside it, the windows bathing them in soft light.

The contrast between the unbroken table and chair and the rest of the furniture was jarring. I frowned, still unable to sense anyone or anything nearby. I stepped into the room, treading carefully as I worked my way through the debris. I got close enough to the table to see two items on it.

A thermos flask and a coffee mug.

My eyes fixed on the steam wafting in the air above the mug.

I sucked in a gasp.

I wasn't alone.

I spun around, and slammed into a hard body, the air forced from my lungs.

Strong arms wrapped around me.

I stiffened, sure it was the orderly who had gone on the run with Dr Wood who had hold of me.

I looked up, expecting to see his menacing face.

Instead I met a crisp green gaze, the bright hue reminding

me of freshly cut grass after a spring shower of rain.

Ethan Rhodes.

I'd found him.

Exultation rushed through me as I smiled up at him, gazing into his eyes. Flecks of gold filled the green, with a hint of brown around the edge of the iris. As I watched, the brown edges thickened before streaking through the green, accompanied by a rumble beneath my feet.

Energy thrummed in the air around us, and my eyes widened as the rich earthiness I associated with the earthquakes filled my senses.

I was right. He was the source.

I reached out to him with my mind, to see if he could hear me like Andie and Celeste, my greeting slamming into the wall I'd encountered before.

He grimaced, arms tightening around me, and I let out a silent gasp when his mental wall pushed my overture away. The floor shifted, and I clung to him, glancing sideways when the flask rolled off the table beside me, coffee slopping over the sides of the mug.

Heavy items fell to the floor in the kitchen area as the quake continued.

Ethan was holding me so tightly it was almost painful, his face twisted into a grimace as he fought to control his power. I could feel his heart pounding and I focused on the feel of his muscular chest beneath my palms. He hadn't allowed me to speak to him mind to mind, but I would do what I could to help him.

I sent a soothing stream of energy directly into his body, letting it wind its way through his system, stroking tense muscles. I sensed the moment he regained a semblance of control and released his hold on the earth.

He exhaled, the beat of his heart easing as his arms

loosened around me. His eyes were green once more, clear, though a frown creased his brow as he stared down at me.

I chanced a gentle touch, mind to mind, and his eyes widened.

'It's okay,' I said, 'I'm here to help you.'

A strange expression filled his eyes before they narrowed. He moved his hands to my elbows, clamping my arms to my sides.

It was my turn to frown, though I tried to soften it with a smile. 'Please, let me go. I won't hurt you. I just want to help.'

He didn't reply to my mental voice, and made no move to release me, though I knew he had heard. But before I could call him on it I felt a sharp sting on my shoulder. I looked to the left and a cold shiver swamped my body at the sight of Dr Wood with an empty syringe in her hand.

She was looking at Ethan, who still had hold of my arms.

My head spun, as whatever she had injected me with made her words to him sound muffled.

'Well done, Ethan. That's one down, and two to go.'

5

Head aching, eyes stinging, thoughts foggy, I forced my head upright. My stomach churned and I swallowed rapidly as I worked to keep the contents inside where they belonged.

I attempted to shift position, to place my hands on my stomach to help quash the nausea. I couldn't move; my arms were somehow pinned to my sides. I forced my eyes to open, vision bleary as I looked around. I was still in the dining room, strapped to the only chair to survive the destruction within the estate.

Horror swept through me, nausea intensifying, breath coming in gasps as I remembered seeing Dr Wood. I rocked backward and forward, struggling to get free. I could not let her imprison me again.

Blackness hovered at the edge of my sight, threatening to carry me away, and I fought to remain conscious. With teeth gritted, I stamped on my panic, forcing myself to think. I could not afford to lose it.

Dr Wood had said something to Ethan before I'd passed out. One down, two to go. She was going after Andie and Celeste. Fear for them helped steady my nerves.

I had to stop her.

Warn them.

All my twisting, trying to loosen the straps securing me to the chair, failed.

They didn't budge, secured just as tight as the ones Dr Wood had used to strap me down whenever she wanted to experiment with my abilities. I delved deep within my consciousness, searching for the spark of my abilities to use it to free myself. It was there, but it slid out of my mental grasp each time I reached for it. I groaned at the tell-tale sign the drug I'd been injected with was still in my system. Bitter experience told me I wouldn't be able to access my abilities until it wore off completely.

I slumped back, hair covering my face. I tossed my head to get the long strands out of my eyes, wincing when the movement worsened the ache behind them. I closed them, forcing my breathing to settle as I cast out my mind, trying to connect with Andie. I might not be able to break the straps, but maybe the drug's effect had lessened enough for me to contact her via our telepathic bond.

She was too far away, my mental voice too weak to project beyond the dining room. It did allow me to sense I was not alone. Someone was in the room with me, their presence muted, like something was blocking me from connecting with them.

But this time I knew what it was.

The wall that Ethan had wrapped around his abilities to lock them way.

I opened my eyes and twisted my neck to look around the room. I couldn't see him, but knew he was somewhere close by. Watching me.

I gave up looking for him with my eyes and used my mind to feel for the confines of his mental wall. He was directly behind me, deliberately staying out of my peripheral vision, his wall masking the earthy scent of his ability. But this close it would not allow him to block out my mental voice.

'I know you're there,' I said. 'And I know you can hear me.'

I sensed him shift position, confirming my suspicion he

could indeed hear my mental voice, just like Andie and Celeste. His unique abilities had opened a channel between us, mental wall or not.

'Please, Ethan, help me. We need to leave this place, before Dr Wood comes back.'

He remained silent, but I got a waft of his scent. Then it was as if he hardened his thoughts to shut me out.

I persevered, refusing to accept this response.

'If you won't untie me, at least call the police. They'll arrest her and make sure she can't hurt either of us ever again.'

His scent flared once again. I was getting through to him.

'She has tortured so many of us, but we can stop her from hurting anyone else,' I said.

A loud snort came from behind me. 'Dr Wood hasn't hurt me. The tests she runs are to help me. She's trying to fix whatever Celeste did to me. She's going to make me normal again.'

I froze, stunned by the anger in his voice.

Ethan stalked out from behind me, arms crossed in front of his chest, his anger a palpable presence in the air around us. The ground rumbled with it. I sucked in a breath when the gaps in the wall he'd barricaded his abilities behind widened, the scent of his mind strengthening as his control wavered.

I shook my head, conscious of the rattle of pots and pans in the kitchen behind me as his anger increased the intensity of the mini quake centred under the estate. 'I'm sorry you think having psychic abilities makes you abnormal. But it's not true. It's a part of who we are. And Celeste didn't make you this way. Your abilities must have been latent. They were just awakened when you touched her.'

'You're lying. I'm not one of you. Celeste did this to me. I am not a freak.'

The rumble in the ground below us deepened, his anger forming further cracks in the mental wall. An image flashed into my head, of a wild and unchecked garden set amidst a forest shrouded in shadows, the foliage arching toward the gap in the wall that allowed a brilliant flash of golden light to shine through.

The chair I was strapped to moved sideways as the floor shifted, and loud bangs sounded nearby as numerous items crashed to the ground.

'Okay, okay. It's all right.' I sent a wave of reassurance toward him, heart aching to see the way the foliage strained toward the light, flowers blooming as if sensing my touch.

As the equivalent of a mental hug reached Ethan, some of the tension leached from his rangy frame, though his frown remained.

'What are you doing?' The cracks in his mental wall sealed over with his words, repelling my broadcast and cutting off my view of the untamed garden that was the spiritual embodiment of his abilities.

'I'm sorry I upset you,' I said, keeping my expression neutral. 'I just want to go home.'

He uncrossed his arms and moved closer, the mini earthquake he had set off fading away along with the last scent of his power, even as his eyes filled with regret. 'I'm sorry too. I really am. But I can't let you go. Dr Wood said she needs all three of you before she can work out how to fix me. She'll let you go again once she's done that, I promise.'

I wanted to protest; to tell him he didn't need to be fixed. There was nothing wrong with him and he was deluded if he thought for one second that Dr Wood would let any of us go, him included. But his emotions were so volatile, and he clearly had little control over his abilities.

Somehow, perhaps as a means of self-preservation or

denial, he had managed to create a mental wall to lock his abilities away. The brief glimpse of the garden and the accompanying scent were evidence of his abilities attempting to break free. From what I'd just observed, this clearly happened anytime he got angry or upset. If he continued to deny this innate part of him the garden would wither and die.

But as much as I wanted to get him to open up, to accept his abilities as a part of him, there was no telling what would happen if I set him off. The violent earthquake from my dream could become a reality if he got so angry he lost control completely and couldn't lock his abilities away again.

I would have to bide my time and hope for an opportunity to make Ethan accept his abilities, to see them as a good thing. Only once he had done so would it be safe for his wall to come down. The image of the flowers in the garden straining for the light suggested that once he was in complete control of his powers, he would be capable of amazing things, and I hoped I would have the chance to experience them alongside him.

'Good, you're awake. Now we can get started.'

I stiffened at Dr Wood's voice, unable to repress a shudder when I looked to the doorway and caught sight of her. The hulking orderly, Karl Sypher, who had often helped to hold me down so Dr Wood could complete her torturous tests, was at her side. They marched across the room to stand beside Ethan. For the first time I could remember, Dr Wood was not wearing a lab coat, her dark coloured slacks and blue blouse creased and covered in what appeared to be dust. Her hair was pulled back in a tight ponytail, but her face showed signs of three months on the run from the police.

She gave Ethan an indulgent smile, tapping him on the shoulder. 'Thank you for watching over Angel. You can go and rest now. It won't be long until we have the other girls, and I'll be able to help you get better.'

'No, please don't go.' Terror drenched me in a cold sweat at being left alone with Dr Wood and Karl.

At my silent plea Ethan glanced at me, brows creasing, before he faced Dr Wood. 'I don't need to rest. I'd like to stay.'

Dr Wood gave a nod and Karl gripped Ethan's shoulder. He shook off the arm, moving back a step to glare at the orderly. The soft rattle of the kitchen utensils sounded, anger loosening his control of his ability.

Dr Wood's caring expression slipped for a moment, but then she rallied and gave a light laugh. 'My dear boy, I'm just trying to do what is right for you. You may not feel tired now, but the testing required to determine how to reverse whatever it was my daughter did to you will take a lot of energy. We'll soon have Andrea and Celeste back, so you need to make sure you're well rested. You wouldn't want to delay further testing because you weren't physically up to it, would you?'

Ethan's frown deepened, and I resisted the urge to shout to him, mind to mind, that she was lying. His control was so thin I didn't want to tip him over the edge. No matter how terrifying I found the thought of being alone with Dr Wood and the orderly, I feared more what would happen if Ethan's wall were to fail completely before I'd had a chance to work with him.

I swallowed my dread as I watched the changing expressions rolling over his face. He clearly wanted to stay, my obvious fear creating a chink in his certainty regarding Dr Wood's intentions, but it warred with his intense desire to be normal. While I could sympathise with him, sure it would be a huge shock to one day be knocked unconscious and then wake up with the ability to set off earthquakes, I hoped his conscience would win out in the end.

My shoulders sagged when he gave Dr Wood a slow nod and avoided looking at me as he moved back. Mouth dry, stomach clenched, I watched him walk out of the room. It took every ounce of mental strength I had not to scream for him to come back.

He'd made his choice, turning his back on me.

Now I had to deal with the consequences.

6

'He's going to cause trouble,' said the orderly. 'You should have let me knock him out.' He held up a syringe he'd been hiding behind his back.

'Nonsense, Karl. The boy worships me. After all, I'm the one who is going to cure him.' Dr Wood gave a hard smile.

'What happens when he realises you've been lying to him, that all those tests to determine the extent of his abilities were so you can use him for your research?'

'By then it will be far too late for him to do anything about it. My research will be made public knowledge.' She shrugged. 'He'll be free to do whatever he wants after that.'

'You know the media will be all over these kids once you go public. They'll be hounded for the rest of their lives.'

Despite the image Karl's words created, his voice was cool, detached, as if he was only bringing it up to make a point. He didn't care what happened to Ethan or me. If he did he would never have agreed to work for Dr Wood once he realised what her methods for testing her research subjects entailed. No one with a good conscience could stand by while she electrocuted children.

Although, it didn't sound like she had used that technique with Ethan. If she had he would surely hate her as much as I did.

'That is none of my concern. The public deserves to know what kind of freaks are living amongst them, and I've worked too hard to let a bunch of teenagers get the better of me.' She leaned over me, a grim smile on her face as she placed her hands on my thighs and dug her nails in. 'You hear that, Angel? I will not let anything stand in the way of achieving my goals. Not you, your family or my ungrateful daughter.'

I glared back at her, making sure every ounce of disgust I was capable of showed in my eyes until she stepped back. The fabric of my jeans had protected me from being cut by her nails, but I was sure her punishing grip would leave bruises.

'Karl, get me the whiteboard. It's time Angel tells us what we need to know.' She moved around me and loosened the strap on my right side, pulling my arm free.

I sought the spark of my abilities, hoping enough time had passed to allow me to finally access it, wanting to lash out with my free hand. It responded, sluggishly but it was there. I sucked in a breath, ready to push Dr Wood away from me.

An electrical current slammed into my right leg. I opened my mouth and let out a silent scream, body shaking as the volts travelled throughout my body. The current stopped as suddenly as it had begun, and I slumped forward, tears filling my eyes, limbs still twitching.

Dr Wood gripped my chin and lifted my head with one hand, holding up the slim Taser she had shocked me with. 'That's just a small taste of what I'll do to you if you don't cooperate.' She let go of my chin and shoved a whiteboard marker into my right hand, forcing my fingers to close around it.

Karl appeared on my left and propped a small whiteboard on my lap.

Dr Wood, still holding my hand, took the lid off the marker and directed it over the board. Then she released my hand and stepped back, reaching behind her to scoop something off the table that the flask and mug had been sitting on earlier, the spilled coffee still smearing the top of it.

'We need to send your sister a message, to ask her and

Celeste to join us. So,' she said with a cold smile, 'what is the password for this?' She held up a mobile phone.

My mobile phone.

She moved to my side, and placed the Taser against my leg. 'On the count of three. Give me the password.'

I shook my head, bracing myself for what would happen next.

Dr Wood wasted no time in responding. Lips pursed, she hit the button to switch the Taser on. I gritted my teeth, eyes screwed shut, riding out the agonising wave of volts slamming through my body, not wanting to give her the satisfaction of seeing how much it hurt. But I could do nothing to stop the silent screams pouring out of me.

'Stop it! You're hurting her.'

The pain ceased at Ethan's shout, though the effects of Dr Wood's torture lingered for a long moment, making my leg muscles twitch. I lifted my head and blearily focused on Ethan as he crouched in front of me. He gently stroked my cheek, wiping away my tears, before he moved back and confronted Dr Wood.

'You said you just needed to question Angel. You didn't say anything about electrocuting her.'

Dr Wood plastered an insincere expression of contrition on her face. 'I'm sorry you had to witness that, but it really is the only way to get her to cooperate. She's been brainwashed by her sister, and my daughter. I must break down the barriers they have created, to get her to open up to me again. We need the password for her phone.'

She placed her hand on his arm, giving a gentle squeeze. 'I won't be able to cure you if I can't study all three of the girls. All I want to do is to find the cure and give you your life back. If Angel won't help us of her own free will, then using this is the only way to get what we need from her.' She held up the Taser.

Ethan shook his head, shoulders back, tremors in the ground showcasing his anger and confusion. 'No. It's not right. I won't let you hurt her again.' He took the Taser out of her hands and threw it to the ground, stomping on it with a booted foot.

'Ethan, you stop that nonsense right now.' Dr Wood's voice was shrill.

Ethan didn't stop until the Taser was in pieces. Chest heaving, he stared her down. 'No cure is worth this.' He turned his back on her and faced me, determination in his gaze. 'It stops now.'

Hope swelled in my heart.

He was going to save me.

I straightened up as best I could, preparing myself to help him free us both, wincing at the ache in my nerve endings with even the tiniest of movements.

I pushed the pain aside. I had to focus if I wanted to escape with Ethan.

He dropped to his knees in front of me, taking my free hand in both of his, eyes locked on mine.

'Please, Angel, tell me the password. I know you think you're protecting your sister and your friend, but Dr Wood is just trying to help all of us. Give me the password so she can find the cure and make all of us normal again.'

My hope leached away, fresh tears stinging my eyes. He wasn't going to help me. All he cared about was the promise of a cure that didn't exist. I was on my own.

'I will never tell you the password,' I broadcast to him, pulling my hand free. 'Dr Wood can torture me all she wants. I will not betray my sister or Celeste. And you're crazy to trust her. She'll turn on you the moment she gets what she wants. I heard her tell Karl, when she sent you away before.'

45

He went still, a torrent of emotions covering his face, disbelief chief amongst them. I knew he didn't want to believe what I was saying. He had pinned all his hope on a cure, and nothing I said would sway him.

He firmed his lips and narrowed his eyes before reaching up to cup my face with his hands. He leaned in so close I could clearly see flecks of gold and brown swirling in the depths of his green eyes. I tossed my head in an effort to dislodge his grip, but he held tight.

'What's the password, Angel? Think about the password and everything will be okay.'

The colours swirling in his eyes increased their speed, pulling me in. I wanted to close my eyes or look away, but I was frozen, mesmerised. I lost myself in his gaze, forgetting everything but the feel of his hands on my face, the light puff of his breath on my lips as he moved even closer.

I didn't breathe, couldn't blink as the soft murmur of his voice called to me.

We hadn't moved, his mental wall still in place, but it felt as if I hovered on the edge of the garden, golden light spilling around me, the plants and flowers beckoning for me to join them. I so wanted to let go and allow my spirit to be refreshed in the soft shadows of his innermost sanctum.

He abruptly released me, leaving me feeling bereft when the glimpse into the garden vanished along with his touch. He wiped his hands on his jeans as he stood and turned to Dr Wood.

His voice expressionless, he said, 'The password is 179342.'

I could finally blink, shaking my head to clear the daze as his words sank in. Somehow, while I'd been entranced by his eyes, lost in the garden, he'd delved into my mind and found the password. I watched on in horror as Dr Wood congratulated him even as she started to type my password into my phone.

No. I would not let her win.

Anger burned away the last of my daze as I reached for the smouldering spark inside me, catching hold of it, and sending out a wave of power to knock the phone from her hands. The shock on her face went a long way toward soothing my anger, but I was not done. I did the mental equivalent of Ethan stomping on the Taser, hammering the phone into the floor until pieces of it were scattered everywhere.

Dr Wood spun around, hand raised to slap me.

Ethan caught her by the wrist and pulled her away from me.

'Calm down.'

'Don't you dare tell me to calm down!' She wrenched her arm free, attractive features twisted into a hateful mask. 'We needed that phone. Andrea would suspect something was up if we sent her a message from a different number, and it's not as if we can force Angel to call and leave her a message. She's mute.'

'It's not the phone that matters,' said Ethan, crouching to poke through the debris of my phone. 'It's the Sim card.'

My stomach lurched when he held up the tiny chip that contained my virtual world. It had to be damaged, after what I'd done to the phone, surely?

I couldn't take the risk. I readied myself to lash out with my abilities.

A familiar sting in my arm set my head reeling. Karl stepped back, the syringe he'd been ready to dose Ethan with earlier now empty.

I fought to stay conscious, mustering up what energy I could to fight the drug in my system the way Celeste once had. My head tilted sideways, eyes closing of their own volition. I forced them to open, watching as Ethan slipped the back off his phone and swapped the Sim card.

It took everything I had to remain awake and aware.

Wind rushed through my head, deafening me. Not that my lack of hearing was an issue. The look of delight on Dr Wood's face when Ethan handed the phone to her said it all. The Sim still worked. They had my password. Nothing was stopping them from sending Andie a text and pretending it was me.

Dr Wood, phone in hand, marched out of the room with Karl at her side, leaving me alone with Ethan.

I let my eyes close and my head droop even more, trying to keep my mind blank. I needed him to leave so I could focus everything I had on purging the drug from my body. When Celeste had done this, it had felt like a fire sweeping through me. I'd used external flame to keep Dr Wood at bay before, but this was different. Now I was sending the flames spiralling through my veins.

Ethan crouched in front of me once more, letting out a soft sigh as he tried to lift my head. 'I'm so sorry, Angel. I hope one day, when Dr Wood has cured us all, you can forgive me. But I had to do it. Don't you see that?'

I made no move, no sign I was aware of him, hiding deep within myself.

Eventually he stood, silently watching me.

After an eternity, he turned and walked away.

Even then I did not move, waiting until the fire I'd set free within my body had completed its task. Only once I was sure every trace of the drug was gone did I open my eyes.

7

They had failed to retie my right arm.

I took full advantage of their lapse to undo the strap pinning my left arm to my side. Within minutes I'd also untied the ones around my torso and legs.

I got to my feet, grabbing hold of the back of the chair to steady myself when my head spun with the change in position. The drug might be out of my system, but getting rid of it had depleted my energy levels. I didn't have time to recover. There was no telling what Dr Wood had sent to Andie, while pretending to be me. She and Celeste could be on their way here right now.

I had to get out of the estate, and warn them.

Ignoring the ache that speared through my head, I reached out, searching for Andie's thoughts. But my body's weakness still hampered my mental voice. I had to get closer, catch her before she arrived at the estate, to have any hope of reaching her mind to mind.

I stumbled to the door of the dining area, listening intently for signs Ethan or Dr Wood and the orderly were nearby.

All was silent.

I crept down the hallway toward the common room, hesitating on the threshold. The quickest way would be to head for the front door and then down the main driveway. But if any of the doors between here and there were locked, I had no power to spare to get them open.

Perhaps it would be better if I left the same way I'd entered, through the garden. It would take longer, but then there would be only one more door I would have to get open.

Either way, the longer I stood there worrying about which way to go, the more chance of discovery there was. Before I could second guess myself, I headed for the back entrance, stepping lightly to avoid making a sound or tripping over the items strewn over the floor.

The rushing noise was back in my head, as was the dizziness. I couldn't hear anything else over it and had to keep one hand on the wall as I made my way down the hallway toward the back door. It was open, and the wild garden, similar to the one I'd briefly glimpsed behind Ethan's mental wall, was visible through it. I focused on the greenery and riotous flowers, breathing ragged as I forced my feet to keep moving.

The effort to rid myself of the drug had taken more of a toll on me than I'd first realised, but I would not, could not, stop.

'What do you think you're doing?'

I froze, heartbeat stuttering at the sound of Dr Wood's voice. I spun around, flattening myself against the wall, but could see no sign of her.

'I'm just checking to see if the police found my stash,' said Karl. 'I've got buyers lined up, and I've run out of the last lot you got for me.'

'I told you to stop selling steroids. We can't afford getting caught by the police because of your little side business.'

'My little side business is what's been keeping us fed, Joanna. You and your circus freaks haven't made us a cent since those girls got this place shut down.'

'Once we get hold of Andrea and Celeste you'll never need to sell steroids again. The girls, and Ethan, are going to make us famous.'

The two of them were in one of the storerooms, the door

wide open. There was no way I'd be able to sneak past without being seen. I would have to backtrack and head for the front entrance after all.

I tiptoed back to the common room, still hugging the wall. By the time I reached the door that led to the reception area, my head was spinning, and my legs felt as though they were going to give out on me at any moment. I pushed on, getting a momentary surge of energy when I saw the door was open. In my current state, there was no way I'd have been able to force the lock.

I let go of the wall and tottered toward the door, eyes fixed on the opening.

A dark shape emerged on the right of me. I caught a glimpse of green eyes and black hair as I careened into Ethan, despair sapping the last of my strength.

I collapsed, his strong arms the only thing stopping me from hitting the floor.

He cradled me against his chest. 'It's okay, Angel, I've got you.'

I struggled to free myself, my efforts as effective as a newborn's would have been. He just held me tighter, calling out for Dr Wood.

There was nothing I could do. I couldn't save myself, let alone stop Andie and Celeste from getting caught in whatever trap Dr Wood had devised for them.

I let my eyes close. I had to rest, and regain my strength. Weakness making me limp, I couldn't concentrate enough to take in what Dr Wood was saying when she reached Ethan's side. I felt myself being carried for a time, before being laid down on a cold, hard surface. The rumble of an engine and the vibration in whatever I was lying on suggested I was in the back of a van.

Gentle hands smoothed my hair back from my face, Ethan

murmuring a soothing reassurance as he lifted my head into his lap. So strange, that I could feel safe in his arms, even though he was aiding my enemy. But that was a conundrum I would have to sort out another time. Cast adrift by exhaustion, I focused on regaining my strength so when we reached our destination I would have a chance of freeing myself.

In my trancelike state, it was impossible to gauge how much time had passed before the vibration of the engine ceased. Light flooded the back of the van when the door was opened, and as Ethan lifted me out I felt the warmth of the sun on my face. I kept my eyes closed, though I was feeling better than I had earlier and could now concentrate on what was being said around me.

'Want me to take her?' Karl asked.

I couldn't repress a shudder at the thought of the orderly touching me, and Ethan's arms tightened around me. 'No, I'm good,' he said.

I sensed Dr Wood looming over me, the acidic scent I'd always associated with her tickling my nose. I held back a sneeze, not wanting her to realise I was awake.

A familiar sting in my upper right arm brought tears to my eyes, even as I waited for the drug to take effect.

'You shouldn't be drugging her again so soon after the last lot. You said it's dangerous.' Ethan's tone was accusatory.

'Relax, Ethan, this is just a light sedative to keep her calm, to prevent her from tossing fireballs around while Karl and I retrieve her sister, and my daughter. Don't let her angelic appearance fool you. Angel is capable of creating maximum destruction. Now, why don't you take her to the end room, and make her comfortable on one of the beds. And don't forget to strap her down,' said Dr Wood. 'We don't want her getting loose again. If you let her escape a second time, all hope of a cure goes with her.'

Ethan said nothing in response though I felt myself being carried, soon losing the warmth of the sun. My head lolled against his shoulder, the sedative Dr Wood had injected me with filling me with a false sense of peace. It was hard to remember he was aiding my enemy, to not snuggle closer and enjoy the simple pleasure of being in his arms.

His footsteps echoed around us, each step making it harder for me to remember why I should be alarmed at my docile behaviour. I fought to open my eyes to see where we were, to resist the lethargy sweeping through my veins, and the peculiar comfort that came from being held by Ethan.

A low chuckle vibrated through his chest, the sound of it making me breathless. 'I know you're awake and, I've got to say, I'm not hating holding you either. Although, I'm pretty sure it's the drugs making you feel that way. Once they're out of your system you can go back to hating me.'

My cheeks flushed as I finally managed to force my eyes open. His green gaze met mine, a smile lurking around the edges of his full lips. I fought the pull of his eyes, focusing on what he'd said instead of my embarrassment at him being able to read me so easily. He seemed calm, so this would be a good time to work on getting him to accept who he really was.

'I don't hate you. I just wish you would listen to me,' I said. 'But it's not too late. We can leave, right now, before Dr Wood comes back. There is so much I want to share with you, if only you'll let me.' I held off on directly mentioning his abilities, instinct suggesting a slow approach was best.

His arms tightened around me, and his gaze turned sombre. 'You know I can't let you go. I need you, for the cure. And trying to run away again would be dangerous. The drug the doctor uses has a mean kick, and now that she's added a sedative to the mix, you could really hurt yourself.'

I stiffened at his mention of the drug Dr Wood used to subdue my abilities. Ethan was helping her, taking part in a trap to ensnare Andie and Celeste, and here I was lying in his arms like some weak-kneed damsel in distress.

If he was not prepared to listen, and continued to toss aside my offers to help him, then that made him my enemy just as much as Dr Wood was. Not that he felt like the enemy. The image of the garden appeared in my mind. It called to me, offering the promise of sanctuary; one he was determined to destroy.

I pushed against his chest, thrashing my legs. 'Put me down.'

'Hey, stop that. You'll make me drop you,' he said as he carefully set me on my feet, keeping his arms around my waist. 'You're still too weak. You need to let me help you.'

I brushed hair out of my face and glared up at him. 'I don't need your help. What I need is for you to let me go.'

'I'm sorry, I can't do that. Not yet. But it will be fine. Dr Wood will fix us both. You'll see.'

'I don't want to be fixed, and you shouldn't either. You just need to learn how to control your abilities and everything will make sense.'

He frowned. 'I don't want to learn. The tests Dr Wood makes me do, so she can determine the extent of the problem, are bad enough.'

Tests. My stomach somersaulted, the word taking me back to when Dr Wood had made me predict what card she was holding up, or the word she was thinking about, administering an electric shock any time I got it wrong. If Ethan had been subjected to the same tests, that would explain how he had been able to pluck the password to the Sim card out of my mind. Yet he still continued to think she was trying to help him.

Before I could form a coherent reply to his ridiculous belief in Dr Wood and her intentions, he had scooped me up and plonked me on a rickety bed with a metal frame. I flailed my arms as he attempted to tie a strap to my left wrist, using his superior strength to pin me down. The sedative meant my fight was ineffectual and he soon had one arm secured and started working on the other.

'No, please don't do this. I'm begging you.' I strained to lift my upper body off the bed, to keep fighting, groaning at the effort it took to even move my head. I lay back down, exhausted, tears filling my eyes.

'I'm sorry it has to be this way, Angel, but you need help.' He secured my arm to the bed rail and moved to wipe my tears away.

I tossed my head and glared at him. He backed off, hands going to the pockets of his jeans. 'You need to cooperate, or you'll only make it harder for yourself. You don't want Dr Wood to drug you again, do you?'

It was an effort to shake my head, but I managed. The last thing I wanted was to have any more drugs pumped into my system. I had to be ready to escape, to prevent Andie and Celeste from being captured, and to do that I needed to be rested and alert. My only hope was that my body would quickly shake off the concoction of suppressant and sedative, allowing me to access my abilities once more.

'Good. I'm glad you're being sensible about this.'

To stop myself from broadcasting what I thought about being sensible, I looked around the room. I was on the bed at the end of a row of six, with a second row of six beds on the opposite wall, all of them looking the worse for wear. The paint on the walls of the large room was cracked and peeling, covered in dust and grime. Not the kind of environment in which I would have expected to find Dr Wood.

'What is this place?'

'This is the main dormitory of an old orphanage. It was shut down decades ago, apparently, and all the buildings have been sitting here empty ever since. Karl said it had a bad reputation, for what happened to the kids who lived here, so no one wanted to have anything to do with it once it was shut down.'

I shuddered to think about what kinds of things might have happened to the poor children who had been sent to live here to have the orphanage gain such a bad reputation.

'Have you been here the whole time?'

He nodded. 'It's not exactly a luxury hotel, and this building is the best of the lot of them, but it is close to the estate. It's well off the main road so not many people remember it's here. The police never came near the place, though we could easily see them combing over the estate. I saw you and your friends there this morning, too, but Dr Wood was out with Karl so I couldn't do anything about it.'

Well, that explained the feeling I'd had of eyes on me. 'You have a wall, blocking off access to your abilities. That's why I couldn't sense you, when you were watching me. Did you know it hid you from me?'

He grimaced. 'I haven't understood a damn thing since Dr Wood's daughter infected me with whatever it is that turns people into freaks. All I know is, I got knocked out and freaky stuff happens when I get angry or upset. But if this mental wall you say I have can hide me from other freaks, then I guess it's a good thing.'

I shook my head. 'You weren't infected, and the wall is only going to work for so long before it collapses completely. You need to learn to control your powers before that happens or the following earthquake will be a hell of a lot stronger than the ones spilling out now.'

The tests Dr Wood was making him do would not be enough to stop that from happening. He needed real training, from someone who understood what it meant to have psychic abilities. But he was so sure having abilities made him abnormal, he would continue to discount my warning. Still, I had to try. Though I decided against mentioning the garden I'd glimpsed behind the wall, or my fear it would wither and die if he continued to deny his abilities. It was such an integral part of him I had the feeling if it died he would too.

'Think of all the good you could do with your powers, if you would just let me help you learn to use them properly. It is because you have a psychic ability that you are able to hear me when no one else can. You can't possibly think that's a bad thing, for someone who is mute to finally be able to have their voice heard.'

His gaze softened, and for a moment I thought I'd got through to him. But then he frowned. 'Dr Wood has never mentioned telepathy being one of the symptoms. All her tests in mind reading were focused on getting me to determine what image Karl was looking at, not actual communication.'

I struggled to sit up, forgetting I was strapped down. The straps dug painfully into both wrists, but I ignored the pain, eyes fixed on Ethan. 'Please don't tell her. It's the only part of me she hasn't managed to corrupt with her experiments.'

He looked toward the door, taking a step backward. 'I have to tell her. She needs to know, for the cure.'

'Please, Ethan. It wouldn't help her with the cure anyway.' I swallowed down my distaste at using his hope of a cure to gain his attention. 'I can't read minds. All it lets me do is talk to people who have arcane abilities like me. You have no idea what it is like to finally have someone able to hear me, after so many years without a voice. Don't let her ruin that for me.'

He turned back to face me, a troubled expression on his face. 'I won't tell her, for now, unless I feel she needs to know for the cure. But you must stop thinking what you can do is normal. It's not. We're not. No one should be able to create earthquakes with their mind, or set things on fire just by thinking about it. This is a disease, and we need to help Dr Wood find the cure.'

On the verge of tears, I smiled sadly at him. 'She doesn't want to cure us. She wants to use us. Don't you get it? We're just science experiments to her. A means to an end. She will torture us, manipulate our powers, and then use the data she collects to regain her standing in the scientific community.'

He shook his head. 'You'll see. Once the others get here, you'll finally realise Dr Wood has been trying to help you all along. If you hadn't run away, if your sister hadn't turned you and Celeste against her, we'd all be cured by now.' He turned around and strode out of the room before I had a chance to say anything more, closing the door behind him.

8

After three failed attempts to reach Andie telepathically, I gave up, still too weak to push my mental voice beyond the room I was held in. I couldn't even tell if I was alone in the old dormitory, unable to sense the life spark of Dr Wood and the orderly, or feel Ethan's presence. For all I knew, the three of them could be standing on the other side of the closed door, silently watching and waiting for their trap to be sprung.

Other than the rickety beds, there was nothing else in the room, no way to tell how much time had passed since I'd first been taken by Dr Wood. The windows were so covered with grime only thin rays of sunlight were able to penetrate the glass. Andie and Celeste could be on their way here right now.

Or worse, captured.

The only hope I had was for Andie to catch on it wasn't me sending the text messages designed to lure her and Celeste to wherever it was Dr Wood planned on snatching them from. I couldn't imagine it would be at the estate as that would be a red flag to Andie that something was wrong. No, it would have to be somewhere else, with a reason convincing enough to get them to leave Daniel and Nick behind.

My eyes widened. What if Dr Wood had a plan that included all four of them? Celeste was the only one with actual powers. If she was neutralised, it would then only be a matter of subduing the others. Daniel and Nick were tall, fit guys, but Karl was a brute and he wouldn't hesitate to cause damage to my brother and his friend if they got in his way.

I didn't even know for sure if it was just Karl who continued to work for Dr Wood. She could have employed any number of unsavoury types to aid in her plan.

Head spinning, thoughts going in circles, the not-knowing ate away at me.

I tugged at the straps, but Ethan had done a good job of securing them. With my abilities neutralised, I was trapped.

It was frustrating to just have to lie there, waiting for something to happen, marshalling my strength. It felt like a major triumph when I was finally strong enough to cast my senses out of the room. Still too weak to contact Andie, I focused on searching the rest of the orphanage. There was still no sign of Dr Wood or Karl, but I did encounter a familiar presence in the room next to mine.

I called out to Ethan, begging him to release me.

He heard me, I knew he did, for I got the impression he was moving. In moments he was outside the door to my room, but the doorknob did not turn. He stood on the other side for a long moment before my sense of him grew fainter.

Minutes, hours, time bled together. The room grew darker as the day sped on. Exhausted from repeated attempts to contact Andie, or get Ethan to listen to me, I drifted off into a fitful sleep. For once I didn't dream about an earthquake drawing me back to the estate.

Instead I stood in the middle of the garden that represented Ethan's arcane abilities. But this was not the beautiful, wild garden I'd glimpsed previously. Instead of a glorious display of flowers of all colours and shapes, the stench of rot filled my nostrils, every plant dead or dying at my feet.

I gazed about me in dismay, one hand covering my nose. Ethan stepped out of the shadows, the smell of rotting plants growing stronger as he trampled them beneath his boots. He stopped in front of me, expression cold and remote, arms crossed in front of his chest. I reached out to him with both my hands and mind, but he backed away to be completely swallowed up by the darkness.

In the dream I fell to my knees, tears streaming down my cheeks as a massive earthquake hit. Heavy piles of dirt rained down on me as the walls bordering the garden cracked open, burying me amongst the dead and rotting plants, suffocating me when I struggled to find air.

I woke with a gasp, eyes gritty, mouth dry, the dream lingering in my mind. Had it been prompted by my inability to reach Ethan with my pleas or was it an ominous portent of what would happen if I failed to reach him?

Ethan's mental wall would inevitably fall, and if I couldn't get through to him, get him to accept his abilities for the gift they were, his power would create a destructive earthquake the likes of which the world had never seen. If that were to happen, for Ethan to realise how much pain and anguish he had caused, the result to his psyche would be catastrophic.

'Angel, where are you?'

I stilled at Andie's voice in my head, scanning the darkened room. She'd sounded close, but I couldn't see her.

'I'm in a building that used to be a dormitory for an old orphanage, somewhere behind the estate, but I don't know exactly where it is,' I said.

'I know where you are. I meant which room are you in?'

Elation had me smiling. 'I'm on the ground floor, in a room at the end of the hall toward the back of the dormitory.' My smile fell. 'Be careful, Dr Wood and the missing orderly are looking for you.'

'It's okay. Daniel and Celeste are keeping watch for them. Nick and I are at the back of the building now. We're going to get you out. Keep talking to me so I can narrow in on your signal.' Her mental voice was strong, vibrant, yet there was a trace of the worry my disappearance had caused threaded through it.

Eyes on the door, waiting for it to open, I asked, 'How did you know I needed you? That I was here?'

'She called me Andrea, in one of her text messages. You know I hate that name, after having Bill and Joyce ram it down my throat for fifteen years. You'd never call me that. And she used proper words and complete sentences. I mean, who does that in a text?'

I swear I could "see" Andie shaking her head at the very thought, and was sure she could read my amusement as I said, 'Grammar issues aside, that still doesn't explain how you found me.'

The door finally opened, and I grinned when Andie, with Nick one step behind, entered the room. She rushed over to me, while Nick remained by the door as look-out.

'When I couldn't connect with you, and neither could Celeste, we knew for sure something was wrong,' she said as she set to work on the straps tying me to the bed. 'She wanted Celeste and me to drive to an abandoned service station on the highway heading west. I played along, pretending I believed you were having some kind of female crisis, and promised to leave the guys at home.'

She helped me sit up, bracing me while I adjusted to being in an upright position, using our bond to talk to me the whole time.

'But instead of going there, we pulled off the road about halfway between the estate and the service station, hiding Daniel's car behind an old shed. When we didn't show up for the meeting, she kept texting me. I fobbed her off, saying we'd broken down and would get there as soon as we could.

Soon after I sent the last text, telling her we were waiting for a car repair guy to show up, we spotted her in a van being driven by that brute of an orderly. I'm guessing they were coming to find us, thinking we really were broken down and fair game.'

Andie's smile dimmed. 'We watched and waited to see where they went, thinking they were going to head to the estate, but they pulled off on a side road and we lost track of them. But thanks to good old Google, we could check out what else was in the area, and found this place. Soon as I got close enough, I could feel you.'

She shook her head, worry once again broadcast along with her mental voice. 'I reached out to you straight away. I could see you, but couldn't get through. It was as if I was watching a movie where you were trapped under piles of dirt, with the missing patient, Ethan Rhodes, watching on. It freaked me out, I've got to tell you, but I kept trying until I finally got hold of you, and here we are. Now, it's time we got out of here, before Dr Wood figures out what we're up to.'

I slipped off the bed, pleased when my head spun only slightly. What rest I'd had, even if a bad dream interrupted it, had helped to restore most of my energy levels. But I didn't think I'd be able to muster up any powers just yet, not until the combination of drugs I'd been injected with had fully left my system.

As much as it thrilled me that Andie had seen through Dr Wood's trap, a heavy feeling settled in the pit of my stomach. It all seemed so easy, too easy, as though they'd been led here on purpose. What better way to spring a trap than to have the prey think they had outsmarted the predator and were home free?

Even if that wasn't the case, I couldn't leave without Ethan.

For Andie to have shared part of the dream, it had to be a foreshadowing of what would happen if I couldn't reach him.

'We need to find Ethan. He needs my help.'

I could feel the wave of disapproval colouring Andie's thoughts. 'After watching him stand by doing nothing to help while you were getting buried, I'm not exactly feeling helpful where he's concerned.'

I clutched her arm as she pulled me toward the door. 'You don't understand. It was a vision, I'm sure of it. Something really bad is going to happen if I can't get through to him. He thinks he's a freak and his powers are caused by an infection, something he believes Dr Wood can cure. But he's wrong. She'll torture him, just like she did us, and when she does, he'll lose control completely and bury us all.'

Andie stifled a sigh. 'I get that you want to help this guy, but it can wait until we're clear of this place. You're not going to be able to help anyone if you get drugged and tied up again because we delayed getting our butts out of here.'

She didn't give me any more time to argue, gesturing for Nick to take hold of my other arm. They pulled me out into the hall, picking up speed as they headed through a rabbit warren of hallways toward a back door. We were almost there when Ethan stepped out in front of us.

'Let Angel go,' he said, glowering when Andie shoved me into Nick's arms and stepped in front of us.

'I'm taking my sister out of here, and you are not going to stop me.' Hands on her hips, she faced him down.

His eyes narrowed. 'You're not going anywhere,' he said. 'Not until Dr Wood has developed the cure.'

Andie gave a snort. 'She doesn't want to cure you. She wants to use you. The same way she plans on using Angel, and I will never let that happen.'

Andie stretched out a hand toward me, offering me the

well of power that resided deep within her, all without taking her eyes off Ethan. 'Move aside, right now, or Angel will blast you out of our way.'

He smiled, though it failed to reach his eyes. 'She's too weak. She won't be blasting anyone.'

'Oh yeah? Show him, Angel.'

I drew on the power hidden inside Andie, taking just enough to restore my vitality and burn away the last vestiges of drugs in my system. It felt wonderful to once again have full access to my abilities. But I didn't use them to blast Ethan.

I eased out of Nick's arms and side-stepped Andie, not stopping until I was right in front of Ethan. I put a hand on his arm. 'I don't want to hurt you. I want to help you. Please, come with us before it's too late.'

'It's already too late,' he said, lifting his chin and indicating something behind me.

I slowly turned around, the ball of dread in my stomach starting to churn.

Dr Wood held a syringe poised against Daniel's neck, while an unconscious Celeste lay sprawled in Karl's arms.

'I'm so glad you could join us, Andrea,' said Dr Wood. 'I was beginning to think you weren't smart enough to figure out my hidden message, the one that led you right where I wanted you.'

'What the hell are you talking about?' Andie, fists clenched at her sides, placed her back to the wall, gesturing for me to join her.

I shook my head, not wanting to move away from Ethan just yet, still hoping I could get through to him.

Dr Wood shrugged, a satisfied smirk on her face. 'I was sure if I worded the initial text message right you would realise something was wrong and come charging in to save your sister. I've had people watching you, informing me of every action you've taken for the last week. All I needed was the right opportunity, which Angel gave me this afternoon.'

Still caught up in the realisation my earlier fear about her having more people working for her than the orderly had been well founded, I remained silent when she turned her smirk my way.

'It really wasn't smart of you to visit the estate on your own my dear, but I'm glad you did. It made snatching all three of you so much easier and more discreet than what I was planning. Now I just need to ensure your bumbling brother doesn't interfere with my plans once again.' Before the last word was out of her mouth she jabbed Daniel in the neck with the syringe.

He recoiled, hands coming up too late to ward her off. Moments later, the drug entered his system and he lurched over to the wall, seeking to prop himself up. Eyes fluttering, he toppled sideways, fell to the floor and was still.

Andie's scream echoed in my head as I reached deep within myself, holding out my hands as a ball of fire flared between them. Eyes fixed on Dr Wood, I prepared to do to her what I could not bring myself to do to Ethan.

9

'Angel, please don't do it.'

Ethan's touch on my shoulder was gentle, not seeking to control me, but to urge caution. Concern radiated off him in waves, making me shiver with the intensity of his emotions.

'You don't have to do this,' he said. 'Dr Wood is not a threat to us; can't you see that?'

Dr Wood stepped closer, but she hurriedly backed off when I raised my fireball higher. She blanched at the implied threat but soon rallied, plastering on an expression of concern.

'Listen to him, Angel. I only want to help, but I can't do that if you insist on fighting me every step of the way. All I've ever wanted to do is help those unfortunates who have been inflicted with psychic abilities; to make them normal again. I know you think my earlier methods were extreme, but I was only doing what I thought best. For all of you.' She waved a hand to indicate Celeste and Andie, as well as Ethan and me.

'Extreme?' Andie scoffed, anger making her voice harsh. 'You tortured Angel and Celeste for years. You tried to torture me, and the only person you're interested in helping is yourself. You're a monster.'

I shifted position, so I could keep an eye on both Ethan and Dr Wood. Nick had moved to stand beside Andie, clearly ready to leap to her defence if need be. Muscles tensing, I prepared to turn my fireball into a wall of fire, to force her to retreat. I would not let her torture us again.

The orderly placed Celeste on the ground and stepped up

beside Dr Wood, the menacing look in his eyes promising trouble. He leaned in close and whispered something in her ear. Her responding smile chilled my blood. She gave a sharp nod and in one split second everything changed.

The orderly put a hand behind his back and produced a pistol which he pointed at Daniel, lying helpless on the floor between us.

'Unless you want to see your brother's brains splattered all over the wall, you'd better put that fire out right now, girl,' he said, mouth twisted into a snarl. 'I'm not joking around here. Because of you lot, I've had to go on the run from the police, leaving all my shit behind, and camp out in this dump for three months. Three stinking months in a rat-infested shit pile with wonder boy here whining on and on about how hard done by he is. Well I got news for the lot of you; it's time for you and the rest of the circus freaks to start earning your keep.'

'What are you doing with a gun? Are you crazy? That's not necessary.' Ethan stepped forward, hands out, panic wreathing his features. 'I'll make Angel see reason. She'll help Dr Wood find the cure. They all will. Just put the gun down.'

Karl gave a bitter and twisted laugh that sent shards of ice into my stomach.

'Listen to you, still thinking you're going to be cured. There is no cure, dumb arse. Once a freak, always a freak.'

'No. What are you saying?' Ethan's head swivelled from the orderly to Dr Wood. 'Tell me it's not true. Tell me he's lying.'

The desperation in his voice doused my flames more surely than anything else would. I placed a hand on his arm. He was wound up so tightly he could explode at any minute. I tried to reach him, mind to mind, sending out soothing thoughts. I could sense the storm brewing inside him as he sought to make sense of what was going on.

The earthquake was sudden but not unexpected, given his emotional turmoil. The decaying frame of the old dormitory groaned as the foundations rocked far beneath us. Cracks appeared in the walls on either side of the hallway, and parts of the ceiling fell, showering us with decades of accumulated dust and debris.

Ethan's gaze was wild. 'Tell me the truth or I swear I'll break open the ground beneath this place and bury the lot of us.'

Dr Wood shot the orderly a foul look before replying. 'Calm down, Ethan. That's not what Karl meant. He's just angry, and lashing out after my daughter tried to electrocute him. Of course I'm trying to cure you. After seeing firsthand what Celeste is capable of, I am more convinced than ever that this is the right thing to do.'

Ethan hesitated, the intensity of the earthquake lessening slightly.

I wanted to urge him not to listen to her, to make him see he was being lied to once again, but with the building already about to collapse on top of us, I couldn't take the risk. It hurt to have to swallow down the torrent of words I wanted to hurl at Dr Wood for putting me in this position. But I did it and cautioned Andie to do the same, releasing my hold on Ethan's arms to use sign language to warn Nick of the danger.

His eyes went wide, and he grabbed Andie around the waist. 'We need to get out of here, before the roof caves in on us.'

'Indeed,' said Dr Wood, 'I do believe it is time to move to more comfortable surroundings. Ethan, could you lend a hand over here and carry my daughter outside?' She gave Nick the evil eye and tossed her head in Daniel's direction. 'You can take care of your friend while I have a little chat with Angel.'

Ethan hurried over to pick Celeste up, careful not to bang her head as he headed for the front door. Nick, with Andie's help, was picking up Daniel. Andie cast me a worried look. I gave her a nod, urging her to leave, assuring her I would be right behind her. After a hurried command from Dr Wood, the orderly stalked off after them, gun pointed at their backs.

Once we were alone, Dr Wood put her hands on her hips and loomed over me, a cruel smile curving her lips. 'I'm sure I don't have to tell you how badly this could have turned out. Unless you want Ethan to lose what little control he has and create an earthquake that will destroy the entire state, I suggest you do what you're told. And before you get any ideas about taking me out or making a run for it, Karl will shoot you. I may need you alive for my research, but a bullet wound or two shouldn't affect the outcome. Then again, it might not be you who gets shot.'

A sinister light lit her hazel eyes as she loomed over me. 'Do you really want to see your brother, or his friend riddled with holes? If you don't promise me right here and now that you will do your best to cooperate fully with my research, then I have no reason to keep them alive. Their continued good health is contingent on your good behaviour, as well as that of your sister's and my daughter's. Make no mistake, Angel, I will do whatever it takes to ensure my research is successfully completed, no matter how many bodies I have to bury to get it done.'

Hands clenched, it took effort to not call back my fireball and throw it in her smug face. But I couldn't risk it. With Celeste unconscious, and Ethan on the wrong side, there was no way I was strong enough to go up against a gun. I also didn't doubt her threat to kill anyone who got in her way was real.

If I could help Ethan to overcome whatever it was that had him walling up his powers, I'd have a better chance of getting him to see through the web of lies in which she'd entangled him. Once his powers were stable and he had no reason to protect her, I would be able to wipe that smug smile away for good.

For now, I could do nothing as she led me toward the front door while casting anxious glances at the ceiling. She exhaled in a rush when we stepped outside. Dusk had arrived while we'd been holed up inside the dormitory, blanketing the abandoned orphanage with shadows.

A mountain range loomed at the back of the orphanage, with trees hemming in a dozen ugly grey buildings. Built for function and not aesthetics, they came in a variety of sizes, linked by cracked concrete paths that were riddled with weeds. In some places, the paths had completely disappeared beneath the foliage.

The exteriors of all the buildings were weathered, with numerous broken windows and holes in roofs. It looked and felt like a ghost town, and I doubted it had been any more inviting when the orphanage had been in operation, not with rusted bars on all the windows. There was no sign of a playground or any other area where children might have been allowed to play. With the way the buildings and paths were laid out, it put me in mind of a giant ugly spider with the building I'd been held in caught in its web.

I shivered at the thought, glad to be outside, but my relief faded at the sight of Karl with his gun pointed at my family and friends.

Ethan, still holding an unconscious Celeste in his arms, glared at the orderly. Perhaps I could use his dislike to seed doubt in his belief in Dr Wood's so-called cure.

'Ethan, if you wouldn't mind leading the way to the

medical building,' said Dr Wood. 'Karl, I'd like you to walk behind us, to make sure no one gets any stupid ideas about making a run for it. You have my permission to shoot them if they do.'

Fists clenched at my sides, I was helpless to do anything when Dr Wood latched on to my arm. 'You can walk with me, so I can keep an eye on you.'

She gave a tug, but I resisted for a moment, once again getting the feeling someone was watching me. It was exactly the same feeling I'd got when I'd been at the estate that morning. I'd thought it was Ethan, as he'd admitted he'd seen me, but he had already set off down one spoke of the path toward a smaller building. Besides, the sensation of being watched came from afar.

I cast out my senses, searching the rest of the dilapidated buildings for the hidden watcher. I knew they were there, got the sense they knew I was aware of them, but that was all I could decipher. Somehow, they had managed to cloak themselves from me in a manner that felt similar to Ethan's mental wall. The hidden watcher's wall was focused on keeping me out, not locking unwanted powers in. I could sense the strength of their abilities, though there was no clue as to what they might be.

Dr Wood said she'd had people watching us for the last week. Was the mysterious observer one of them? It was hard to imagine someone else with the same kind of abilities would be out there now and not be connected in some way to Dr Wood.

Karl gave me a hard shove in the lower back, bringing me back to myself, and I let Dr Wood pull me along with her as we hurried to catch up with Andie and the others.

The building we were walking toward was in far better condition than the ones either side of it, and showed evidence of recent repairs. Bright light streamed out of unbroken, clean windows that gleamed behind shiny new bars.

'I'm afraid we won't be as comfortable here as I would like, but it will serve its purpose seeing as you lot made it impossible for us to return to the estate,' said Dr Wood as Ethan reached what looked like a brand new front door, complete with electronic keypad and numerous locks.

'Why would you want to go back to the estate? There's nothing there,' Andie said over her shoulder. 'The police cleaned all your files and equipment out, and it's been sold. Pretty sure the new owners wouldn't like you using it to torture teenagers and do sick experiments on them.'

Dr Wood gave a low chuckle. 'That's what I like about you, Andrea, always direct and to the point. But with the estate gone, and seeing as my daughter saw fit to steal all my money, I had to find backers who were willing to foot the bill to see my research project completed. In return for being made silent partners, they agreed to set up a new facility, here, where no one will ever think to look for you.'

Andie gave a loud snort. 'Celeste didn't steal your money. You stole hers. You had her committed, so you could get your filthy hands on her trust fund.'

Dr Wood's face twisted into a snarl as she glared at Andie. 'That money should have been mine. If I'd known her pathetic father was going to leave his entire fortune to her, I would never have gone through with the pregnancy. I only married him in the first place to gain a new surname and a level of anonymity after the debacle in Sydney.'

Ethan shot her an appalled glance, and I hid a small smile. Perhaps he was finally starting to see her for who she really was, a monster. But if he had second thoughts about what his role in this was, he didn't say anything as he changed the way he was carrying Celeste so he could stretch out a hand to press the button on top of the keypad.

Before he could touch the intercom button, two armed men in black uniforms appeared from either side of the building, rifles pointed in our direction as they closed in. Ethan backed up toward us, head swivelling as he tried to keep an eye on both guards as they moved to block the doorway.

'State your business,' one of them said, expression grim as he looked over our small group.

Dr Wood let go of my arm and strode up to him. 'For heaven's sake. You know exactly who we are. Now unlock the door and let us in.'

At another time, I might have enjoyed seeing her so put out, but the sight of two more guards appearing from the sides of the building had my stomach churning. They trampled the weeds under their booted feet as they got into position behind us. The sight of all the crushed foliage reminded me of the dream I'd had of the rotting garden hidden behind Ethan's mental walls, surer than ever that it had been an omen of things to come.

The sickening feeling in the pit of my stomach intensified when the door finally opened and a tall man in a white lab coat stepped outside, two more armed guards at his back. They swiftly moved to join their counterparts, boxing us in, rifles at the ready.

Just who had Dr Wood gone into partnership with?

10

'So, this is Angel, the prodigy child.' The man in the lab coat, half his face obscured behind a bushy beard and thick glasses, rubbed his hands together. 'I have been looking forward to studying this one.'

I could feel his eyes on me, skin crawling at the avaricious emotions coming off him in waves. The sting of it set my eyes watering but I made no move to dry them, not wanting to appear weak. As it was, I felt like a meal being paraded in front of a lion.

Ethan moved to my side, his arm bumping against my shoulder. 'Angel isn't here to be studied. She's here to be cured, the same as me.'

The scientist or whatever he was looked taken aback. He shot a sideways glance at Dr Wood, and then gave a forced laugh. 'Of course, young man. Of course. Well then, I'm Dr Frankel, and I believe it is time we got you settled inside and started work on that cure of yours.'

He stepped to the side and indicated for Ethan and me to enter the medical building. The armed guards shifted to form an aisle for us to walk through, eyes hard as they watched us. I couldn't move, frozen in place at the thought of what might await us once we were inside.

Fierce waves of protectiveness were coming from Andie, and I knew she was prepared to do whatever it took to defend me against this new threat. But I could also feel her fear. We were seriously outnumbered, not to mention outgunned, with no way of knowing what new nightmare Dr Wood had dragged us into.

I chanced a quick glance behind me to give her what I hoped was a reassuring smile. Nick was at her side, carrying Daniel. Karl shoved past him, an insolent grin on his face as he strode down the aisle of guards, gun still in his hand.

I craned my neck to see where Dr Wood had gone and saw she was deep in conversation with Dr Frankel. From the look on her face, she was not happy with whatever it was he was saying to her.

A thrill of apprehension raced down my spine. From what I'd observed so far, her financial backers had no intention of playing the part of silent partners, and it terrified me to think of how that might affect us. It had been bad enough when it had just been Dr Wood we'd had to worry about. This new group were clearly well funded and had prepared for trouble if the armed guards were anything to go by. But who were they expecting trouble from?

It was crazy to think they would go to such extremes on our account. Psychic abilities or not, we would be no match for trained guards.

'Get moving,' said one of the guards, gravelly voice filled with menace. I had no doubt he would make me move if I didn't immediately do as ordered.

I forced my feet into action, Ethan at my side, frowning when I stepped through the door and found myself in a tiny reception area. Bare of furniture, faded wallpaper hanging in shreds from the walls, dust and debris covering the floor, it was as uninviting as the old dormitory. The windows here were still original, covered in grime, dimming the outside light. But there was enough to see Karl disappearing through a doorway at the back of the room.

The doorway led to a narrow hall, bright light spilling around the edges of the half-open door at the end. Dust kicked up by our feet filled the air as I forced myself to move toward it. Karl reached the door and opened it fully, his bulk blocking my view of what was on the other side. He finally stepped aside when I shuffled in behind him and I gasped at what I saw.

The walls weren't in any better condition than the ones in the front room, but that was the only similarity. Dr Wood's partners had been busy renovating this area, having set up a circular observation desk in the first part of the room. It was curved so the two women in lab coats seated on stools behind the counter had uninterrupted views of the treatment rooms lining the back wall.

There were four rooms in total, all in a row, with large windows cut into each one to allow the medical staff to see inside. Sawdust and tools were spread on the floor, suggesting they had only just been completed, though there was no sign of any workmen. The female scientists' eyes lit up when they saw me, and I got a whiff of the same avaricious scent as Dr Frankel put out.

I was pushed farther into the room as the others crowded in behind me, retreating to the wall as Dr Frankel strode up to the circular desk and swept a clipboard off the counter. 'We didn't have a lot of time to set this up, so I'm afraid your accommodations are rudimentary,' he said, as he indicated for Karl to take Celeste from Ethan.

'How long do you think it will take until the cure is ready?' Ethan moved forward and clasped my hand. Though he was technically the enemy, his touch helped to steady me.

Dr Frankel gave Ethan a smile that contained zero warmth. 'Well, young man, that depends on how cooperative you all are. The program will run much more smoothly if you and your friends are willing to accept the important role you are to play in helping to shape the future of mankind.'

His eyes travelled over the rest of us. 'Now then, let's get you all settled in for the night. We have a big day of testing planned for tomorrow, so I want you all well rested.' He waved a hand and one of the women behind the counter hit a series of buttons that disengaged shiny new locks on all four doors. They swung silently open, gleaming traps waiting to snap closed on us.

I'd sworn I would never let Dr Wood cage me again, but these four rooms were purpose-designed to imprison research subjects, and with six armed guards standing at our backs the odds against a successful escape had increased exponentially, but so had the potential danger if I allowed myself to be locked up.

I would have to bide my time and hope that when Celeste woke and was able to add her power to mine, I would have been able to get Ethan to accept his abilities and switch sides. Without his help, I could see no way in which any of us would escape whatever fate Dr Wood and her new partner had in store for us.

'Dr Frankel, where do you want us to put them?' One of the armed guards, grizzled face blank, gestured at my family and friends and me.

'Let's see,' said Dr Frankel, stroking his beard. 'I think it would be best if each of the ladies had a room to herself for the time being. The young men will have to share a room until we decide exactly what part they are to play.'

He turned to Dr Wood. 'If that's all right with you? It's your research program, after all.'

Dr Wood lifted her chin, a sour expression in her hazel eyes. 'Yes, it is my program. But I agree the girls should be separated. Celeste is bound to cause trouble when she wakes up. I want an armed guard outside her room at all times, as well as Angel's room. I don't care what you do with the young men aside from Ethan. They're of no use to me.'

Dr Frankel waved his hand and four of the guards brushed past me to take up positions beside each open doorway. Then he turned to look Nick and Daniel up and down. An amused gleam showed in his eyes as he said, 'That's a tad harsh. They're healthy young men, and it's clear they have formed strong ties with the young ladies. It would be a shame to waste that.'

His gaze lingered on Ethan's and my joined hands before he said to the remaining two guards, 'Put the young men in Observation Room One. Angel can have the room next to theirs, followed by her sister and Miss Wood.'

'Hey, watch it,' said Andie. The younger of the two guards had latched on to her arm, pulling her away from me, tugging her around the observation desk.

She tried to pull free, but he only tightened his grip. Nick stepped forward to help her, but his efforts were hampered as he still had an unconscious Daniel over his shoulder.

The older guard raised his rifle and pointed it at Nick. 'Stand down, right now. I'm not going to warn you again.'

Dr Wood leaned forward to whisper in my ear. 'Remember what you promised me. Your brother and his friend are expendable. I will order the guard to shoot them both if they refuse to cooperate.'

I let go of Ethan's hand and darted around to stand in front of Nick, and signed, 'It's okay. We'll be okay. Just do what they want for now.' I looked behind him to Andie, sending her the same message.

'Angel, are you sure? If we let them lock us up they will never let us go again.' Andie's words rang in my head.

Squashing down my own fears, I gave her what I hoped was a confident smile. 'We've escaped before. We can do it again, once Celeste and Daniel are awake.' I kept my thoughts

79

tight, focused only on her, not sure if Ethan could hear my conversations with others.

I flicked a glance at him, but his expression gave nothing away as he watched on.

'Out of my way.' Karl shoved past Ethan and trudged into the last room on the right where he placed Celeste on the bed. He pulled the door shut once he exited the room and the display on the keypad lit up to indicate it was now locked.

Not that a locked keypad would be a deterrent once Celeste was up and about and the drug was out of her system. They must have hit her hard and fast back at the orphanage, giving her no time to react, or she'd have been able to burn it out of her system by now.

The orderly stalked up to Nick. 'Your turn.'

After one last long look at Andie, Nick spun on his heel and walked into the first room on the left, depositing Daniel on the bed and arranging him comfortably.

The guard holding on to Andie didn't speak as he dragged her to the room beside Celeste's, and with my caution ringing in her head she didn't fight him. Soon the door closed on her, but though we had been separated, I took comfort from the fact we could still communicate telepathically.

Now it was just Ethan and me left.

'You're next, wonder boy,' said the orderly as he gestured for Ethan to enter the room with Daniel and Nick.

Ethan went rigid. 'What? No. I'm not one of them.'

He backed up as the two guards shifted position, focusing their weapons on him. 'Tell them,' he said to Dr Wood. 'Tell them they don't need to lock me up.'

I heard an unspoken 'again' and shuddered at the pain it held. He was remembering the aftermath of the emergence of his latent powers, when he had no idea what was happening to him. He'd unconsciously called out to me soon after, when I'd returned to the estate to find proof to have Dr Wood arrested. I'd been exhausted, powers drained, and hadn't recognised his cry for help for what it was.

How different the last few months would have been if I'd understood, if I'd only taken the time to investigate further. I'd have been able to help him come to terms with his abilities, stopping him from locking them away behind a mental wall. Instead, I'd left him in Dr Wood's hands, allowing her the chance to gain his trust and warp his reasoning.

Now the guards were moving to either side of him, ready to lock him up with Daniel and Nick. Perhaps this was the moment when he would finally realise how wrong he'd been to place his faith in Dr Wood and a cure she had no intention of creating.

I didn't need the sudden scent of fresh earth to know an earthquake was imminent. The shaking of the floor beneath my feet said it all.

In his confusion, Ethan's control over the wall he'd created to contain his abilities had slipped.

If I couldn't calm him down, fast, he was going to bring the building down on top of us.

11

I lurched forward and gripped Ethan's arm, spinning him around to face me.

He stiffened, trying to pull away, but I held on, reaching up with my free hand to cup his cheek.

'Breathe. Just breathe,' I said, sending out a constant stream of calm thoughts mentally and through touch. His green gaze, streaked through with brown and gold, latched on to mine and I willed him to listen, to let go of the confusion and anger surging through him.

In the background there was the hubbub of many voices talking at once, but I had no time to listen to what they were saying. Every part of me focused on helping Ethan, on getting him through this moment of betrayal. He was losing it, the power welling up inside him preparing to lash out in a devastating blast. I had to calm him down, but how?

Out of time, I let instinct guide me, pulling Ethan's head down and pressing my lips to his. Warmth surged through me as his mouth moved over mine, arms wrapping around me and crushing me to his chest. I had a moment to note a lessening in the press of his power before being caught up in his kiss.

An eternity later, he broke off the kiss, staring down at me with wonder in his eyes. Before he could say anything, Karl emptied the contents of the syringe into Ethan's neck.

Ethan's eyes rolled back in his head, legs crumpling under him. He fell forward, and I wrapped my arms around his torso, his weight sending both of us to our knees. His head fell to my shoulder and I eased him down to the floor, resting his head in my lap.

'Karl, that was not necessary,' said Dr Wood, her tone waspish.

'Sorry, Joanna, but I don't work for you anymore. He's the boss now, and he wanted wonder boy down for the count,' he said, pointing at Dr Frankel.

Dr Wood stiffened, nostrils flaring, eyes narrowed. 'Don't be ridiculous. Of course you work for me. This is my research program.'

Karl let out a harsh laugh as he loomed over her. 'You don't get it, do you? It's not your program anymore. It's theirs. You handed it over to them the moment you took their money. They own you now.'

'They most certainly do not own me. And no one is taking this program away from me. They can't. It's mine.' Her voice turned shrill as she shook a fist in his smirking face.

'Dr Wood, Joanna, there's no need for hysterics. No one is taking anything away from you,' said Dr Frankel, easing his way between them.

He signalled for the two guards not manning the doors to step forward and they positioned themselves on either side of Dr Wood. 'However, it has become clear your lack of control where the subjects are concerned, and the unfortunate matter of the existing warrant for your arrest, have had a detrimental effect on the program. As such, we have decided it is better for you to take on more of a consultancy role, until we can sort out your legal difficulties.'

Eyes fixed on Dr Frankel, she didn't appear to notice the guards flanking her. 'You can't do that. There wouldn't even be a program without me.'

He gave her a cool smile. 'We are well aware of your genius in getting the program up and running, and will endeavour to see you receive the credit you deserve for your contribution once it reaches culmination. In the meantime, you can continue to work with me, as a consultant only. If that is not to your liking, and you would prefer to sever ties with our corporation, and chance the legal system on your own, then you are free to leave at any time. But in accordance with the papers you signed, your research subjects remain the property of the corporation.'

The colour fled Dr Wood's face as it finally dawned on her that she had been effectively outmanoeuvred. Normally this would have made me smile, but the repercussions for those I cared about dowsed any amusement in the proceedings. Dr Wood was a known enemy, her obsession fuelled by a desire to get back at those who had ridiculed her in the past and to regain her standing within the scientific community. Dr Frankel's motives were completely unknown.

But one thing was clear and that was he and his corporation had big plans for Ethan, Celeste and me. Plans that meant we would never be free.

Once he assured himself Dr Wood was suitably cowed, Dr Frankel turned to Karl. 'You can put Ethan in with the other young men while I escort Angel to her room.'

I leant over Ethan, laying my arm over his chest as I glared at the orderly. If he tried to take him from me, I would scorch his hair with a fireball. I had to be there when Ethan woke up, to counter his anger and pain at being betrayed. It wasn't enough to be able to talk to him telepathically, not if I wanted to avert a massive earthquake when his powers were unleashed. Once his wall came down there would be no containing the backlash.

Dr Frankel leaned down, the expression on his face once again reminding me of a hungry lion. 'Now, now, Angel, there's no need to be frightened. We'll take good care of your young man.'

I turned my glare on him, reaching deep within myself to harness my ability to rattle the walls. While I was nowhere near as strong as Ethan when it came to causing earthquakes, I was more than capable of inflicting damage. Alarmed cries sprang up from the two women behind the observation desk as stationery and computers tumbled about.

Dr Frankel's expression hardened as he straightened and looked to Karl. 'Shut her down, now.'

Karl shrugged. 'Used my last dose on wonder boy.'

Dr Frankel spun around and barked at one of the women, 'Get me a sedative before she brings this place down around our ears.'

'Oh, for heaven's sake,' said Dr Wood, pushing Dr Frankel aside to crouch in front of me. 'Unless you want your brother and his friend to suffer for your actions, you need to cut that out right now, Angel. You promised me you would cooperate.'

In the silence that followed my compliance, she gave Dr Frankel a smug smile. 'As your consultant, I would suggest keeping Angel and Ethan together. She has clearly demonstrated the ability to calm him down, which will come in handy once he wakes up and realises he is now your property.'

Dr Frankel stroked his beard for a long moment, remaining silent as he stared Dr Wood down. Finally, he gave a slow nod, turning to the women behind the observation desk. 'Angel and Ethan are now designated Alpha Female and Alpha Male. Please ensure their medical records are up to date so we can smoothly implement the next stage.' He then swung around to face me, a wide smile on his face. 'Congratulations, Angel, you two are the first volunteers for my bio-weapons program. You and your kind are going to change the face of modern warfare.'

Shock rippled through me, and I made no protest as Karl scooped Ethan up and carried him toward the only empty room. Dr Frankel put out a hand to assist me to rise and I scrambled backward, not wanting him to touch me. I lurched to my feet, never taking my eyes off him as I hurried to join Ethan.

The snick of the door closing behind me, and the buzz that signified the lock had been engaged was a relief, creating a barrier between me and Dr Frankel's bombshell. One look confirmed the window beside the locked door only worked one way. On this side of the wall it was a mirror, meaning anyone in the observation area had an uninterrupted view inside the room, while I could not see them.

But I could feel them, standing there, watching as I moved to Ethan's side and arranged his limbs in a more comfortable position than the untidy sprawl the orderly had left him in. That done, I sat on the edge of the bed, hands clasped in my lap, and scanned my newest cell, determined to show nothing of my inner turmoil to my audience.

Andie was calling out to me, the one person guaranteed to see through my false air of calm, and I did my best to soothe her worry without going into detail. The idea of Dr Frankel using us as weapons was horrifying enough to contemplate let alone say out loud, or telepathically in my case.

I forced all thought of the future aside as I got up to investigate the open door in the wall opposite the bed. Once I confirmed the presence of a tiny shower cubicle and toilet, with no obvious sign of a camera, I returned to my perch on the bed to wait until Celeste, Daniel and Ethan woke up.

While there was no evidence of chains, this room was no better than the one Dr Wood had kept me locked up in, and I had no intention of staying here a minute longer than necessary. There was no way in hell that any of us were going to be used in some insane bio-weapons program.

We were getting out of here, and I was going to get immense satisfaction in helping Ethan bury Dr Frankel and his program once and for all.

For now, I could do nothing but wait, barely acknowledging the arrival of a guard with a plate of sandwiches. My stomach rumbled, reminding me I hadn't eaten since breakfast, but I waited until the guard left the room before I took my first bite.

The last sandwich eaten, I headed to the bathroom, vision blurring, head spinning. The sandwiches must have been laced with a sedative. After I'd used the toilet I stumbled back to the bed and stretched out beside Ethan, unable to keep my eyes open any longer.

12

'Angel, can you hear me?' The panic in Celeste's mental voice jolted me awake.

'I'm here. We're all here,' I said, sending out a reassuring wave as I sat up and rubbed my eyes.

'Where is here? Is this the estate?'

I could sense the dread welling within Celeste at the thought of being back in her mother's clutches.

'We're still at the orphanage.' I explained what had happened while she was unconscious, and could sense the fear building inside her with each revelation.

'What are we going to do? I'm so weak I can barely produce a spark. How are we supposed to escape if I can't use my ability?'

'It's going to be okay,' I said. 'We will get out of here. We just need to wait until the sedative has fully left your system, and Ethan's. You and I on our own would have no chance against six armed guards. But with his help we can do it.'

'Do you really think he'll want to help us escape? If he's so determined to be cured, he might not want to leave.'

'I'll convince him.' Surely what had transpired before the orderly had drugged him would make him see there was no cure. Even if he still held out hope once he woke up, I would make him see reason. I had to.

'You like him.'

I stilled at Celeste's words, flushing as I looked to where Ethan still lay sleeping on the bed I'd shared with him.

'I don't even know him. I just want to help,' I said, touching my mouth as the memory of Ethan's lips on mine sizzled through me.

I knew Celeste was smiling as she said, 'Of course you want to help him, but it's more than that. I can hear it in your voice. Does he feel the same way?'

I shook my head, forcing myself to shift my gaze to the blank wall. 'He's confused. Angry. Afraid. He's not ready to feel anything, for anyone, until he figures out who he really is, and accepts his abilities as a gift and not a curse.'

'Well, I hope for all our sakes he figures it out fast. I can sense people staring at me from the other side of this mirror, and their emotions are not filling me with the warm and fuzzies.'

'I know what you mean.' I could feel them too, observing all of us, and I would not give them the satisfaction of acknowledging their presence. Not until I was ready to let them know they could not control me.

'On a plus side,' said Celeste, 'I didn't wake up with amnesia this time. I feel as though I've been run over by ten trucks, but I still remember who I am, so I'll take that as a win.'

I smiled at her attempt at humour before mentally reaching out to Andie. Her response was sluggish, probably from a dose of drugged food, but her mental voice strengthened as we talked. There was no way to contact Daniel or Nick. I could sense their presence in the next room, but the flicker of flame that signified Daniel's spirit was muted, barely more than embers, suggesting he was still asleep.

'So, what's the plan?' Andie asked, and I could picture her standing, legs spread, fists clenched at her sides as she faced the door of her room.

'We wait. There's nothing we can do until we're all awake and able to fight.' Stretching my mental voice so both Andie and Celeste could hear me as well as one another, I filled them in on the plan I'd hastily devised.

'And you're sure Ethan will agree to that?' Andie asked, making no effort to conceal her doubt.

'He has to. It's our only way of breaking free,' I said, letting my gaze travel over his handsome face. He looked peaceful, a trace of the garden scent wafting through the tiny room now that his rigid grip on the mental wall had slackened as he slept. He was capable of so much wonder, and it was my job to make him see that.

As if he felt the weight of my gaze, he stirred, eyes opening slowly. I leaned forward to place a finger against his full lips, feeling the gentle puff of his breath against my skin.

'Don't speak out loud,' I said. 'They're watching us.'

He struggled to sit up and I wrapped an arm around his back to help him.

He blinked several times as he looked about the room. His eyes narrowed as his gaze fell on the mirror, no doubt sensing our watchers.

'What happened?' he asked silently, rubbing his neck.

'You were drugged. Dr Wood isn't in charge anymore. Dr Frankel is, and he has no intention of creating a cure.' Neither had Dr Wood, but I left that unsaid for now. Best to let him dwell on one betrayal at a time.

He jumped to his feet, swaying as the drug still in his system played havoc with his equilibrium.

'We have to get out of here,' he shouted out loud. 'I have to find Dr Wood. She has to cure me. She promised.' He lurched over to the door and started banging on it, calling out for Dr Wood.

I shot to my feet, clutching his arm and turning him to

face me, tears stinging my eyes at the sheer panic radiating from his spirit. I caught a brief glimpse of the garden behind his mental wall, but the drug prevented his powers from lashing out. His agitation set a strong wind blowing through the garden, thrashing the plants about. Dark shadows partially obscured the golden light.

'Ethan, it's okay. It will be okay.' I reached up to cup his cheeks, forcing him to look at me. My eyes met his and I did everything I could to soothe his battered spirit.

He stilled for a moment, and we stood in silence, hearts beating in sync. Then he pulled away from me, fists clenching and unclenching. 'You don't understand. I have to be cured. There is something wrong with me. People got hurt because of something I did, and I can't go home unless I make sure it never happens again.' His words were no less passionate for being spoken mentally.

I sucked in a breath at the anguish in his eyes. 'Ethan, did you have your abilities before you touched Celeste? Is that why you were at the estate?'

He sat heavily on the bed, staring down at his hands as he turned them over to inspect his palms, as if searching for a mark to explain what he could do. 'I almost killed my best friend, and a heap of others, just because I was angry.' He looked up at me, and my heart ached to see tears streaking down his face, mirror to the ones staining his mental voice.

Questions bubbled up in my head, but I held them back, not wanting to halt his words now he was finally talking.

'We were at a party, I'd been drinking, and I got into a stupid fight with this guy over something I can't even remember. All I know is he shoved me, and said something that made me furious. I could feel this wild energy, building up inside of me, and when I threw a punch at him it exploded out of me. The next thing I knew the ground was shaking and the brick wall beside us collapsed.'

He shook his head, eyes wide, lost in the memories. 'Hamish was standing behind me, trying to get me to calm down. He copped the worst of it. The guy I was arguing with and I got out of it with a few bruises and scrapes, same as the other people who were standing nearby. Hamish wasn't so lucky. A large chunk of the wall came down on his head. He's been in a coma ever since, and with every day that passes it's more unlikely he'll wake up.'

I sat beside him, taking his hand in mine. 'It wasn't your fault.'

'That's what the authorities said, that all the injuries were sustained because of a freak earthquake nobody could have predicted. But I knew. I'd felt it, knew I was the cause of the earthquake, knew Hamish was stuck in that hospital bed because of me.'

'Did Dr Wood know you had a psychic ability when you were admitted?' I frowned even as I asked the question, sure his name would have been on the files we'd stolen from the estate if she'd been aware of what he could do before Celeste had escaped.

'No. I kept it a secret; what I'd done. I figured people would think I was crazy if I told them I'd caused the earthquake.' His mental voice had a bitter tinge. 'They did think me crazy, but only because I went off the rails once we found out Hamish wasn't going to wake up. After a month of that I got sent to the estate because my parents figured I was suffering from survivor's guilt. I'd been there five weeks, attending the counselling sessions, saying whatever it was I thought the doctors wanted to hear so they would set me free.'

He shook his head. 'I'd even gone a fair way toward convincing myself it was all in my head, that I'd imagined being able to set off an earthquake. Then I touched Celeste, and well, you know the rest. I blamed her, convinced it was some kind of infection, even talking myself into believing I must have encountered someone like her before the party.'

He straightened, shoulders back, expression determined. 'That's why I need Dr Wood to cure me. It's bad enough I put my best friend in a coma. You saw what it was like, when they said they were going to lock me away. I completely lost it. If it hadn't been for you, and what you did...'

His gaze warmed as he looked at me, then dipped to my lips.

A flush swept over my body when he leaned closer. 'When I think about what almost happened. God, Angel, I could never live with myself if something I did resulted in you getting hurt.'

'I'm fine. No one was hurt, and I can teach you how to control your ability if you will just give me a chance.'

He gave himself a shake. 'I can't risk hurting you or anyone else. I have to be cured. I have to.'

I steeled myself to rip away the security blanket he had been clinging to for the last three months. 'I'm so sorry, Ethan. There is no cure. There never was. Dr Wood was lying to you.'

'No, that's not true. She promised me.'

'She told you what you needed to hear, so you would do what she wanted. None of it was true. She was going to use you, use all of us, to restore her reputation. But none of that matters anymore. We have a bigger problem now Dr Frankel is in charge.' I quickly filled him in on what had happened after he'd been drugged.

His eyebrows rose, eyes wide as he stared at me. 'I won't do it. I won't use my ability to hurt innocent people.'

'Neither will I. As soon as you and Celeste are back at full strength we are getting out of here.'

He was silent for a moment, and then he reached over and took my other hand. 'I've been an idiot. You told me all along that Dr Wood was lying to me, but I didn't listen. This mess we're in, it could have been avoided if I'd just listened to you.'

I squeezed his hands. 'It's okay. You were confused. Upset. I just wish I'd been able to find you sooner, before she got her hooks into you.'

His smile was warm as he said, 'Well, you've got me now.'

I smiled back at him, sure my cheeks were flushing as I asked, 'Are you ready to get out of here?'

He gave a nod and I reached out to Celeste. 'Ethan is awake, but still groggy. How are you feeling?'

'I'm heaps better,' she said, her mental voice filled with grim determination, 'and ready to show these Peeping Toms how wrong they are to mess with us.'

The flickering flame in the next room that signified Daniel's spirit had been growing steadily stronger. He was awake, so that removed one more complication. Now the only thing holding us back was Ethan's weakness.

Steadying my breathing, I focused on the feel of his hands in mine, sending him some of my vitality.

'No, stop.' He tugged his hands free, concern etched on his face. 'You're weakening yourself. I can feel it.'

'It's okay. As soon as I get to Andie I can use her to refuel. Right now, you need this energy more than I do,' I said as I snagged his hands again. The scent of freshly mown grass and rich earth filled the room as his beleaguered spirit soaked up what I freely offered, though his mental wall remained in place.

Once he was able to stand unaided, I called on Andie and Celeste, smiling at the surprise in Ethan's eyes when their voices sounded in his head as well as mine.

'Are you ready for this?' I asked, receiving three firm responses. 'Then let's do it.'

I stepped over to the door and placed my hand on the keypad, sending a probe inside the panel to disengage the lock. The second it started to open Ethan bolted through the gap, the rich scent of his garden filling the air as he harnessed his anger and made the floor rumble beneath us.

A fireball blazed to life between my hands as I followed him into the main room.

13

Celeste had fried the lock to her room and was now working on Andie's. I tossed my fireball toward the observation desk before moving to free Nick and Daniel. The earthquake Ethan had created made keeping my footing difficult, but that was a small price to pay if it kept the armed guards out of my hair. The four assigned to guard duty reacted quickly to our escape attempt, rallying in the middle of the room, raising their weapons.

As soon as she was free, Andie rushed to my side and took my hand, restoring the energy I'd given to Ethan. Filled with power, I sent out a wave of it to knock the rifle out of one guard's hands, while a zap of lightning was swiftly accompanied by a pained cry of alarm as Celeste took care of another.

The two women behind the observation desk were screaming, using whatever was close to hand to try to stem the flames on the counter, smoke rapidly filling the room.

One of the guards had his rifle pointed at Celeste, the other preparing to fire at Ethan.

My rush of power hit the guard aiming at Ethan at the same time as a crack sounded below him. The guard dropped his rifle and hit the ground hard, rolling to the side to avoid falling into the crevasse that had opened up in the floor, while Nick darted in and scooped up the discarded rifle.

The sound of a concussive blast nearby was followed by a scream, and I spun to see Celeste toppling sideways, a bloom of red on her chest.

'No.' I sprang forward, lashing out at the guard who had shot her, sending him flying backward into the wall behind him. He hit with a sickening thud before slumping to the floor and remaining still.

Daniel launched himself over to where Celeste lay on the ground, worry stamped on his face as he lifted her into his arms. 'We need to get her to a hospital,' he said, anguish in his voice.

Nick and Andie raced to his side, and I wasn't surprised to see she had picked up another rifle. She and her boyfriend looked more than ready to use them if anyone tried to stop us. But if the guards were still in a position to fight, they wisely chose not to. Through the smoke I saw two of them pick up their fallen comrade, and head for the door that led outside, the remaining guard cradling his right arm as he hurried to join them.

I called out to Ethan, letting my spirit wrap around his as I helped him regain control over his abilities. The rumble of earth below us gradually eased and he ran to join me. I waved a hand to douse the flames still ravaging the observation desk now they had served their purpose. The women had vanished, and I covered my mouth to shield it from the smoke as we rushed for the door.

There was no sign of Dr Frankel, Dr Wood, or anyone else when we burst out into the light of a new dawn, but I could hear shouting in the distance and knew we didn't have long.

'Where's the van we came here in?' I asked Ethan, dread settling inside me at the pallor of Celeste's face and the shallowness of her breathing. Daniel cradled her to his chest, fear radiating from him.

The silver flicker that represented her spirit was fading, her life force ebbing away as blood poured from the wound in her chest. Nick had pulled off his tee-shirt and Andie had wadded it up and was trying to stem the blood loss, but it was not enough. Celeste was dying.

I hurried to Daniel's side and placed my hand over Andie's. At her hasty nod I drew deeply from the reservoir of power that existed within her, pouring it into Celeste along with every ounce of my spirit I could spare. But the damage done to her internal organs by the bullet was too great. It had passed completely through her body, leaving a trail of destruction in its wake.

All the power Andie and I contained was not enough to save Celeste.

My eyes met Ethan's and I reached out to him with a hand covered in Celeste's blood. 'Please, help us.'

He took my hand without hesitation, gripping tightly as he focused everything he had on the link between us.

I gasped at the rush of power that flowed through me and into Celeste's body, wild and uncontained like the spirit trapped behind his mental walls. Locked away for months, it responded with an eagerness that would have been joyous if not for its current purpose. I'd never felt anything like it, watching in awe as Ethan's confusion melted and the walls surrounding his garden began to crumble.

No longer shut away, the flow of power coming from him increased in intensity. Celeste's body shimmered as it worked its way through her flesh to repair what had been torn asunder.

I could see it all, tears streaming down my face as a healthy glow returned to her cheeks. Within moments she was opening her eyes, blinking up at us in wonder, still part of the connection that had been created when Ethan took my hand.

He staggered, his hand falling away from mine, the connection severed, and I turned to catch him before he fell.

'You did it,' I said, mental voice brimming with pride and awe. 'You healed her.'

He stared at his hands, a thunderstruck expression on his face, the rich scent of his spirit filling the air around him now the mental wall locking the garden away had been destroyed.

He shook his head. 'I don't understand. I break things. I don't heal people.' His gaze latched onto mine. 'It must have been you.'

I shook my head. 'No, Ethan. Don't you see? Your power over the earth comes from nature. It's a gift. One you can use to bring new life.' I waved a hand to where Celeste was gingerly standing, Daniel's arm wrapped tightly around her waist. 'Or restore it.'

Hope filled his gaze. 'Hamish? Do you think I could heal him too?'

My smile trembled. 'Yes,' I said, feeling the truth of it in my heart. Of all of us, Ethan had power with the potential to change the world.

His smile was so bright and full of promise, but it died a second later.

A chill swept over me when I saw the reason.

Dr Wood and Karl Sypher stood in front of us, the orderly holding the gun he threatened us with the day before.

His face a mask of fury, he pointed the gun at me. 'You little bitch. You've ruined everything. Again.' Spittle flew from his lips as he roared at me, and I shrank back as he took aim.

I had nothing left, all my and Andie's combined power spent in the effort to save Celeste. Ethan was equally exhausted. If Karl pulled the trigger now there was nothing I could do to stop him, and no way Ethan would be able to heal me.

'No.' Ethan's horrified cry filled the air as Karl pulled the trigger.

I flinched, expecting at any second to have the bullet rend through my flesh.

A swirl of power, brimming with unbridled strength, brushed past me, forming a shield off which the bullet bounced harmlessly. Before I had time to blink, Karl yelled as the gun was wrenched from his hands by an unseen force, the surprised look on his face quickly overtaken by anger once again.

'You did this.' He pointed at me.

I shook my head and turned to Ethan, but he looked just as surprised as I felt. But if he hadn't saved me, then who had?

Before I could voice my question, a male police officer raced around the side of the medical building and tackled the orderly to the ground. More officers quickly followed, but my gaze was glued to an older man who was calmly surveying all of us.

He looked to be in his mid-forties, fit and tanned, with only a trace of grey in his thick brown hair. Laugh lines crinkled around his eyes and mouth as he said, 'Hello, Dr Talbot. It's been a long time.'

I twisted around, searching for the person he was referring too, frowning when all I found was Dr Wood.

She was staring at the newcomer in horror. 'You,' she said, voice all choked up. 'You did this.'

'Well, I certainly played my part. But the bulk of the credit must go to Constable Carlton. He's the one who organised this welcoming committee for you and your friend there after he was spotted buying steroids in town.' He pointed to where the young constable had Karl on the ground, a knee in his back as he slipped a set of handcuffs over the orderly's thick wrists. A second officer was bending down, photographing the gun with which the orderly had just attempted to shoot me.

Four other police officers stood nearby, one holding a second set of handcuffs ready.

'Sorry, I'm being rude. Allow me to introduce myself. My name is Mark Davidson. I was Dr Wood's original Subject A, only she was using her maiden name then.'

It all sank in. This was the boy who had ruined Dr Wood's career when his psychic abilities were revealed to be fake. Only they weren't. I'd just seen for myself that he had real power, felt the rush of it against my skin.

The officer who had been waiting with the handcuffs moved forward and I heard her say, 'Dr Joanna Wood, you are under arrest for—'

Dr Wood immediately began shouting, trying to dodge the officer, only to be boxed in by two more. She struggled in their arms, her words incoherent as she fought to get away.

'I think it would be best if we left the police officers to do their job,' Mark said over the noise, 'and I'll explain how I managed to show up just in time to save the day while I take you lot home.'

He reached out and tapped my arm as he led us to a 4WD parked out front of the old dormitory and said, 'I'm sorry I wasn't able to stop them kidnapping you at the estate, Angel. I was too far away at the time, but at least I was able to follow when they brought you here. It just took me a while to persuade the police to join in the fun.'

While I would never have classed any of this as fun, what he'd said overrode my misgivings. 'It was you I could feel watching me.'

His eyebrows rose. 'You could sense me, despite my mental shield? You are even more special than I first thought. If that's the case, you will make a wonderful addition to our organisation.'

'Organisation?' I stopped walking and faced him. 'What organisation?'

He glanced around to make sure no one other than my family and friends were in earshot. 'This isn't the place I imagined making my pitch, but here goes. I belong to an organisation dedicated to finding and training those who possess psychic abilities. They recruited me when I was a subject of Dr Talbot's, who you know as Dr Wood. They are the ones who set it up to make me look like a fraud in an effort to prevent word of what people like us can do from spreading to the general population.'

'They faked it?' Dr Wood's reputation had been ruined, fostering her obsession to prove her theories about psychic abilities were correct, and it had all been a lie. It was difficult to comprehend how that one act had gone on to adversely affect so many lives.

Mark continued to talk, oblivious to the turmoil building inside me.

'You have no need to worry about her anymore. Our organisation has taken steps to ensure she is locked away for the rest of her life, and all her talk of people like us will be written off as the ravings of a lunatic. All of you are safe, thanks to our organisation.'

Beside me, Ethan stiffened. 'So, what, now we owe you? Is that it?'

Mark looked taken aback. 'No, of course not. We are aware everything that transpired here is a direct result of what happened in Sydney all those years ago. We're just cleaning up our mess as it were. But, in having said that, we would like the three of you to consider joining our organisation.'

I looked over to the others before I replied. 'The three of us?'

'Yes, you, Ethan and Celeste.' He shot a smile toward Andie, Nick and Daniel. 'I'm sure we could find something for you guys to do, but the organisation is mainly interested in those with psychic abilities.'

I filed away the realisation he didn't know Andie was a reservoir of power, contemplating his offer. He seemed like a nice person, and had just saved my life, but with his mental shield in place I had no way of judging his sincerity.

After a long moment, I said, 'I don't know about Ethan or Celeste, but I've had enough of being wanted for what I can do and not who I am. Dr Wood and Dr Frankel both thought they could use us for their own ends. I'm not ready to sign on with any organisation who wants to do the same thing, no matter how good their intentions are.'

Mark hid his disappointment well as he turned to Ethan. 'And what about you? Do you think the same as your girlfriend or are you willing to give us a try?'

Eyes wide, face flushing, I made to move away from Ethan before he objected to having me named as his girlfriend. But he only squeezed my hand, giving me a reassuring smile before he said, 'I go where Angel goes.'

A warm glow suffused my body at his words, a wide smile blooming as Celeste chimed in to refuse Mark's offer before he could ask her the same question.

It appeared I wasn't the only one who was done with being a research subject.

14

Ethan let go of my hand and approached the still figure lying on the bed, the only sound the slow beeps of the machines monitoring Hamish's vital signs. He pulled the chair closer to the bed and sat, hands trembling as he reached out to smooth the sheet covering his friend's body.

His shoulders shook, overcome with emotion, and it took everything I had not to step forward and offer comfort. Ethan needed to do this on his own, or he would never free himself from the guilt over his part in the accident that had put Hamish in a coma.

It had taken a week for him to be ready to face this, a week in which the bond forged between us by shared adversity had strengthened as I worked to teach him how to control his abilities.

'Hey, mate,' said Ethan, his voice thick with tears. 'Sorry it's been a while since I've been to see you. I kind of got caught up with stuff. I know that's no excuse. I should have been here. The same way you were always there for me. But I'm going to fix it, right now.'

A gentle swirling of his power filled the room with the strength of his love and commitment, the dying flowers in the vase on the bedside table perking up, regaining their colour and bloom. Tears streamed down my cheeks at the visible sight of his growing mastery over his abilities.

'Why are you crying?' The words were soft, scratchy, as if the owner was only now remembering how to speak.

Ethan shot to his feet, wiping away his tears as he leaned

over the bed. 'Hamish, you're awake.'

Hamish's eyes were open, unfocused, as he stared at Ethan. 'Yeah, buddy. I'm awake. No need to shout.' His brow creased as he struggled to move. 'Shit, man, what happened to me?'

'Take it easy,' said Ethan, placing his hands on Hamish's shoulders to still his movement. 'We'll get the doctor.'

I scooted farther into the room, pressing a red button on a keypad outside the private toilet to call for assistance. Within minutes the room was filled with people, with Ethan shunted back from the bed as the medical staff swarmed around Hamish.

Ethan retreated to my side, fresh tears welling in his eyes as he watched them work on his friend. 'I could have done this months ago, when he first got hurt. Instead I ran off and left him lying there.' His mental voice was filled with disgust.

'Ethan, no, you couldn't have helped Hamish back then. You weren't ready. You needed to be able to accept your ability, to see it as a part of you and not a disease before you could learn to harness your healing powers.' I reached up and placed both hands against his face. 'You're a better person today because of what you went through. Every experience, good or bad, has helped to shape the man you are now. A man who can heal.'

I let him feel all the wonder and love I held for him in my heart. He was such an amazing person, and now Hamish had woken from his coma Ethan would finally be able to complete his own healing.

Not that I expected life to be perfect from now on. Dr Wood had been declared clinically insane and committed to a mental health institution, just as Mark had said would happen. But there had been no sign of Dr Frankel. He and his team had fled the orphanage ahead of the arrival of the police, and there had been no trace of him since.

Dr Frankel wasn't even his real name, and the documents Dr Wood had signed to receive financial backing had proved to be fakes as well. There was no telling who he really was or where the funds to set up the medical facility at the orphanage had come from.

He was out there, somewhere, but I refused to let thoughts of what he might be up to taint the joy I found in the company of my family and friends. For the first time in my life I was truly free, and with Ethan at my side I was determined to make the most of it.

Book Two

Blind Sight

1

I gulped in air as I sat up in the hospital bed, chest heaving, pulse racing, eyes clamped shut.

'Concentrate on your breathing, Belinda. You're going to be fine.'

The voice was brisk, matter of fact, one of the many nurses flitting in and out of my room while I recovered from the car accident that stole my sight.

I clutched the coarse blanket covering my lap and shuddered. 'I saw something.'

The nurse gently took hold of my head.

'Honey, that's wonderful. Open your eyes. Tell me what you see.' Her voice resonated with excitement.

I blinked back tears as I opened my eyes and found my sight blocked by a familiar and unrelenting black wall. 'You don't understand. I still can't see anything. But I saw…'

She let go of my head and rubbed my shoulder.

'Aw, honey, it was just a dream. You were still asleep.'

'No, I was wide awake. I wasn't dreaming.'

'You must have been.'

I shook my head, taking in deep breaths and kneading the blanket as I searched for the words to tell her what I had seen. 'There was a woman. I think she was a nurse. It was dark and she was alone in the car park. She got to her car and a man grabbed her from behind. She didn't even have time to scream. He grabbed her and shoved her in the boot, and then he drove away with her.'

'Let's make you more comfortable,' said the nurse.

Seconds later the bed began to vibrate as the back rose. Then she plumped the pillows behind me.

'There, that's better.'

'Weren't you listening? Someone was attacked, kidnapped. Don't you care?'

'I'm sure it must have seemed very real, but there's no way it could be. It was a nightmare. That's all.'

My shudders returned as I pictured the terror on the woman's face when she realised what was happening to her. Was the nurse right? Had it all been nothing but a bad dream? But it had felt as if I was right there, watching it all unfold.

'She had long brown hair, like me, but her hair was pulled back in a bun. And her car was blue, a Commodore I think. It looked new, and the licence plate was JLD01.'

I closed my eyes, not that it mattered, but the action helped me concentrate, to remember more details.

'She had her keys out ready to unlock her car when he grabbed her, and there was a tiny silver disco ball on the keyring.'

'What do you think you're doing? Do you think this is funny? A joke?' Her voice was harsh, angry.

'I'm sorry. I didn't mean to upset you. I'm just telling you what I saw.'

'No you're not. You're trying to scare me. You need to stop it, right now.'

Tears pricked my eyes. 'I don't understand why you're mad at me. I haven't done anything to you.'

'That's my car. The nurse you claim to have seen getting attacked is me.'

'You?' I shook off my shock. 'Then you have to be careful. Someone is going to try to kidnap you.'

'I said stop it.'

'But—'

'No, I'm not listening to any more of your rubbish.'

The door to my room slammed shut as I sat hunched in the bed, bewildered by what had just happened. I sagged against the pillows, nausea bubbling in the pit of my stomach, desperately wishing what I'd seen had been a dream.

But if it was, how could I know what the nurse looked like, or what kind of car she drove?

It didn't make sense. Unless... unless it was real.

The door to my room reopened. I wiped my eyes, hoping the nurse had returned. I'd be able to tell her I thought the dream, vision, whatever it had been, was meant as a warning and not some sick joke.

'Young lady,' said a stern voice, 'I'll not have you upsetting my staff.'

'I didn't—'

'Juanita told me what you did and that kind of behaviour will not be tolerated in this hospital.'

I fought back more tears, voice unsteady. 'I'm not lying. How could I know what kind of car she drives or what she looks like? I'm blind.'

'You obviously had someone help you and if you persist in making up stories or try to play such an awful trick on any more of my nurses, I'll have you moved to another ward.' Having delivered her warning, the woman exited the room, leaving me alone with my personal darkness.

A short time later I heard footsteps in the hallway outside my room and a new voice called out in an overly cheerful tone that it was breakfast time. I listened as the woman placed a tray on the trolley positioned on the right side of my bed and then manoeuvred it in front of me.

'Need help with that, love?'

I shook my head, not trusting myself to speak, and waited for her to leave before I put out a hand to explore the contents of the tray.

I couldn't have felt less like eating. I hadn't had much of an appetite since the day I woke up and discovered another car had taken out me and my Ford Festiva.

But while I wasn't hungry, I was thirsty. Throat thick from fighting back fresh tears I was determined not to let fall, I searched until I found a small container of liquid that was either water or juice. I held it steady on the tray with one hand as I peeled off the lid. Careful not to dribble any down my front, I took a tentative sip.

Apple juice. Gross.

I set it back on the tray and patted the rest of the items until I found the individual serve carton of milk meant for the bowl of cereal, twisting it in my hands as I struggled to open the spout. I tugged at it, but my fingers slipped off and banged into the bowl.

I moved the bowl to the side, frowning when I got a strong whiff of apples. I touched the tray and found a sticky mess coating the bottom of it.

The apple juice. I must have knocked it over when I banged the bowl.

'Oh no.' I shoved the trolley out of the way and pushed the bedding back. Juice had soaked through the sheets, and my pyjamas. 'That's just great. They'll think I wet myself.'

The tears I'd tried so hard to hold back fell in earnest. I wanted to run away, hide, and find somewhere where I could be alone. But I could barely navigate the confines of my tiny hospital room without bumping into something. To go anywhere, do anything, I needed someone to guide me because of my useless, stupid eyes.

I hated them, hated sitting in the dark never knowing what was around me, or if people were looking at me.

'Would you like a tea or coffee, dear?' The voice of the

tea lady came from the doorway.

'I don't want anything. Can't you people leave me alone for five minutes?' I covered my face with my hands and listened to her hasty retreat. Then came a murmur of conversation from the hallway before someone else entered the room.

'Had a little accident, have we?'

Mum's voice was cheery and light. 'Your father will be back in a minute. I've just sent him to the cafe downstairs to grab us a couple of cappuccinos,' she said. 'It will give us a chance to get you all cleaned up. By the time he returns you'll be good as new.'

'I'm sure the hospital said they were all out of working eyes, and they won't be getting any more stock in until, hmm, let's see, when hell freezes over. So I guess I'll never be good as new, will I, Mum?'

'A nice hot shower will do you the world of good. I've got your favourite dress, the cobalt blue one, for you to put on.'

I shook my head, not surprised she'd ignored my comment about the eyes. Dad was the same. Maybe they thought if they ignored me I'd stop saying stuff they didn't want to hear. Well tough, I was blind and ignoring it wouldn't make it go away. If that worked I'd be seeing in full colour.

Brushing off Mum's helping hands, I slid off the bed with the dress bunched in my fist. Made of a soft knit material, in a blue a shade darker than my eyes, it had a full skirt that fell to just above my knees. Whenever I wore it I would stand in front of the mirror, admiring the way it swirled as I twisted and turned.

No mirror in the world could show me my reflection now.

Sniffling back fresh tears, I ran my free hand along the wall leading to the bathroom door and pushed it open.

'Would you like me to come in with you?' Mum asked.

I shook my head, quickly shutting the door behind me, and shuffled forward to the toilet, hanging the dress over the rail attached to the wall before using the facilities. Once I was done, I stripped off my soaked pyjamas and followed the rail to the corner that comprised the shower. Pulling the shower curtain around me, I stood to one side as I turned the taps, waiting for the water to warm up.

Hands skimming over my healing body to avoid placing any pressure on the bruises and lacerations I'd sustained in the accident, I soaped up and let the hot water wash over me.

It felt wonderful to fully immerse myself, washing away the memory of the morning's events.

To finally be alone.

I couldn't wait to get out of there, to not have strangers walk in and out of my room all day, to feel them looking at me and be unable to look back.

After towelling myself dry, I felt for the cupboard under the sink where my underwear was kept and grabbed out knickers and a bra. I'd always made a point of buying matching underwear, but there was no way to tell if what I'd just put on was a set or not. Just one more thing to add to the list of things I'd lost.

I slipped on the dress and brushed my hair, twisting it into a low ponytail. Then it was time for my teeth, and I used a finger to determine if the toothpaste had made it onto the brush. Setting each item back in the same spot I'd taken it from, I took a deep breath and felt for the door handle, opening it and stepping into the bedroom.

I ran straight into someone, their elbow connecting with one of the deep bruises on my torso. 'Ouch.'

'Sorry,' said a voice I recognised as the cleaner. 'Didn't see you there.'

'Great! Not only am I blind, I'm invisible too. This keeps getting better all the time.'

'Belle, the lady is here to clean your room.' Dad spoke from the other side of the room, his gentle rebuke making me frown. 'She's already changed the bed sheets.'

'Good for her,' I said, hands out in front of me to avoid banging into anything or anyone else on my way back to the bed.

I knew I was being rude but couldn't help myself. The woman had been cleaning my room for the last two weeks and couldn't fail to notice I was blind. She should have taken more care not to bang into me. It wasn't as though I could see the cleaner coming to get out of her way.

I waited until she'd left before clambering onto the bed. With my body still tender, it was an awkward process and I hated having an audience for it.

'Why don't you sit in the chair by the window?' Dad asked.

The suggestion, after I'd just made myself comfortable on the bed, irritated me. 'Why would I want to do that?'

'It's not as if you're sick and need to stay in bed, honey. You're allowed to move around. You can even go outside if you want.'

'I don't want to sit in the chair. I don't want to go outside. What I do want is for all of you to stop pushing me.' Since the accident, I'd had a steady stream of people coming to my room and trying to get me to accept being blind. Psychologists. Occupational therapists. They all said it would get better, but I didn't want to get used to being blind. I wanted my sight back, I wanted to feel normal again.

'Honey, no one is pushing you. Your dad and I just want to help.'

'You can't help. No one can, so just leave me alone.' I

laid my head back against the pillows, closing my eyes as I willed them to go away. Instead, I heard them pull chairs close to the bed.

'Do you mind? I'm trying to have a nap here,' I said.

'Belle, you just woke up. How can you be tired?' Dad's tone was tight.

'I guess being blind takes it out of a girl.'

'We drove all the –'

'John, it's okay. We'll leave Belinda to have her nap. She's obviously not feeling well today.'

I bit my bottom lip at the hurt in Mum's voice and wanted to apologise, to dive into her arms the way I used to when I was little and have her kiss away the pain.

But they were heading for the door and I didn't know what to say to call them back. Perhaps it was better they left. It couldn't be much fun sitting in a room staring at someone who couldn't stare back, someone who was in a foul mood. I wasn't ready to let anyone else in and wasn't sure if I ever would be.

I'd had my entire future planned out. Finish my art degree, get a job with a firm specialising in design to get real experience, and then one day branch out on my own.

Now it was all gone. Without eyes that worked, how could I be an artist?

I was useless, a failure. Better to be left alone.

Harsh sobs racked my body as I wished for the umpteenth time this was a nightmare from which I would wake up, bitterly aware no amount of wishing would make my dream come true.

2

The door to my room opened, hitting the wall with a loud bang, making me jump.

The evening session for visiting hours had ended some time ago, not that I'd had anyone come to see me after I'd run Mum and Dad off that morning. No one had been to my room all day other than the silent worker who dropped off my lunch and dinner. Not even the nurses had been back, finally giving me the peace and quiet I'd thought I wanted, leaving me alone to stew in my thoughts.

Smiling at this sign I hadn't been forgotten, I said, 'Hello?'

'Miss Gregory, I'm Detective Johnson from the Easton Police Department. I'd like to have a word with you.'

The detective's voice was hard, cold.

'What is it? Is it my parents? Are they okay?' A shiver swept over me.

'I'm not here about your parents. I'm here about Juanita Daniels.'

I shook my head. 'Juanita Daniels?' Even as I said it, the name sank in. Juanita. The nurse I saw in my nightmare, or whatever it was.

I gasped. 'Is she okay?'

'No thanks to you. She's shaken, and has some scrapes and bruises, but that's nothing compared to what's going to happen to you and whoever you set up to attack her.'

His voice was filled with grim satisfaction, eager to tear me down.

I could feel him looming over me, and I shrank back against the pillows. 'I don't understand. I haven't done anything wrong. I just told her what I saw. I didn't know it was her.'

'You really expect me to believe you had a vision of your nurse getting attacked, a vision that came true?'

'I don't know what it was. A vision. A nightmare.' I ran my hands over my face, shaking my head. 'I didn't want it to happen.'

'Don't give me that bull. You made it happen. Tell me who helped you set it all up.'

'I didn't do anything. How could I?' I waved a hand toward my eyes.

'Being blind doesn't mean you couldn't have arranged this. All it would take is a few phone calls and a friend willing to help out. You got bored sitting in this room all day and decided to have some fun scaring one of your nurses with a fake vision. When that didn't work you got someone to make your vision come true.'

I searched desperately for a way to convince him how wrong he was. 'When? I don't have my mobile phone with me, and you can easily check the calls made in and out of this room and see there haven't been any since I got here. I'm also sure there's a pay phone in the hospital somewhere but how could I find it? There is no way I could have done what you're accusing me of.'

Until now I couldn't have believed my life could get any worse, but here I was being accused of arranging to have a woman attacked. It was crazy.

'I haven't got it all figured out yet, but I will find out how you did this and you—'

Someone burst into the room.

'They caught him.'

The new voice was deep, though younger sounding than the detective's.

'What?'

'He attacked another nurse in the main carpark. Her screams alerted the security guards and they managed to subdue him before he could do anything but scare her.'

'Well then, Miss Gregory,' said the detective, smugness filling his voice. 'If you won't tell the truth, maybe your friend will.'

'He's not my friend. I'm telling you, I had nothing to do with this.'

'We'll see.'

The detective and his partner left, but I couldn't relax. After an hour of lying there with my mind reeling, I used the bedside controls to buzz the nurses' station, hoping to get something to help me sleep.

For two hours I waited for somebody to respond to my call, sitting up straight each time I heard footsteps outside my room. But no one came. No doubt they thought the same thing Detective Johnson did, that I'd set up the attack on one of their own.

Eventually, exhausted, I fell asleep on top of the covers, caught in a replay of the vision of Juanita being attacked, only this time it was me the man shoved into the boot of the car. Finally, I dragged myself back to wakefulness.

As I struggled into a sitting position I realised someone had covered me with a blanket, the scratchy feel of the hospital issue harsh against the bare skin of my arms. Tears pricked my eyes at this small sign of kindness. Maybe not everyone hated me.

My door creaked as it opened. I brushed away the tears and turned to whoever had entered, trying to keep my face expressionless. The person who had opened the door remained silent. I could feel the weight of their gaze and shivered. What if the police hadn't caught the man who attacked Juanita after all? Maybe it was him standing in the doorway, come to wreck his vengeance on me for spoiling his plan.

Goosebumps erupted all over my body and I clutched the blanket close.

'Belinda, is it okay if I come in?'

I recognised the soft voice. It was Juanita, though I'd never heard her sound so hesitant. The nurse had always been firm and staunch in her goal to help me come to terms with my blindness.

I didn't trust myself to speak past the lump in my throat so just nodded and listened to the pad of Juanita's feet as she moved toward the bed. Then came the sound of something heavy being placed on the bedside table. A soft fragrance wafted over me. Perfume?

'I brought you some flowers. I know you can't see them, but they smell beautiful. There are all sorts of colours in the bouquet; the roses are pink, and their buds are just starting to open. The carnations are purple and there are daffodils and chrysanthemums and other things I don't know the names of. I hope you like them.'

The words came in a rush, as though Juanita was tripping over her tongue to get them out.

'Thank you. They do smell beautiful.'

'I'm sorry about yesterday, when I said you were lying. I know you were telling the truth. I don't know how but you saw me getting attacked. You tried to warn me, and I didn't listen.'

It sounded as if she was on the verge of tears, and I didn't blame her. It was a waking nightmare, my vision coming true, the police accusing me of making it happen.

'How come you believe me now?'

'I spoke to the police late last night. They questioned the man who attacked me. He's obsessed with nurses and he'd been watching us all week, waiting until he had the chance to grab someone.'

Juanita's voice cracked and I knew the tears she'd tried so hard to hold back had started to fall.

I reached out a hand, but quickly dropped it. I had no idea what area of her I was closest to and didn't want to touch anything I shouldn't.

'Anyway,' said Juanita, voice deceptively light, 'I just wanted to say thank you. I'll be taking a few days off and you'll probably be gone by the time I come back to work.'

I nodded slowly and could hear her backing away from the bed.

'I'd better go. Your breakfast will be here soon and I know how much you hate an audience.'

I finally found my voice. 'Juanita, I'm glad you're okay.'

'Me too.' The tremor in Juanita's voice said she wasn't too sure if she was okay.

I understood the sentiment as I wasn't sure if I would be okay either.

What was wrong with me?

Wasn't being blind enough of a curse? Did I have to suffer through horrific visions as well?

A short time later a nurse entered the room. 'I need to check your blood pressure,' she said in a curt tone.

She roughly grabbed my arm and slapped on the cuff, all without saying another word.

Until yesterday all the nurses had been extra chatty. While I could understand the nurses being mad at me before, surely Juanita would have explained to them that I had not been behind the attack?

'Did Juanita tell you what really happened last night?' I asked.

The nurse dropped my arm and ripped off the cuff.

'Listen here, you little bitch. You may have fooled Juanita but there are no such things as visions. You made it all up and if you think we're going to let you get away with it you're wrong.'

Suddenly there was a loud crash and drops of water splashed against my arm.

'Oops, I accidentally knocked your lovely flowers over. How careless of me.'

I sat in silence, too stunned to react as the nurse scooped the ruined bouquet of flowers off the floor and left the room. The rattle of the breakfast cart woke me from the daze, unable to comprehend how someone could hate me so much. I fought in vain to stop the tears streaming down my face.

Sunk in self-pity, I huddled on the bed, not moving as the untouched breakfast tray was removed sometime later. I didn't respond to the tea lady's brusque enquiry either. I lay like a stone and wished for the thousandth time that I could wake up from this nightmare.

'Miss Gregory. Can I talk to you for a moment?'

I jumped. I had been so sunk in my misery I hadn't realised anyone had entered the room.

Then I scowled. I knew that voice. It was the police officer who had barged in last night to tell Detective Johnson the man who attacked Juanita Daniels had been caught.

'What do you want?'

'My name is Scott Carlton. Constable Scott Carlton. There are just a few things I'd like to clear up about what happened yesterday… for my investigation.'

'What investigation? I thought you caught the guy. The crazy nurse stalker who has absolutely nothing to do with me?' I gritted my teeth, tensing up as I waited for him to rip into me the way the nurse had.

'We may have caught him, but that doesn't explain how you knew about the attack before it happened. Ms Daniels said you had a vision.' His words were measured, with a curious lilt, as if he didn't blame me. Unlike everybody else. I wished I could see him, to see the expression on his face to help me determine the truth of his words.

'Please, Miss Gregory, it would really help if you told me exactly what you saw.'

He sounded genuine, and some of the tension left my body as I shook my head. 'I don't know what it was. All I know is that I saw it, in here.' I tapped the side of my head. 'When I told the nurse about it, she said it was just a nightmare, but I was wide awake and it felt so real.'

As I haltingly described what I'd seen, I sensed him moving closer to the bed, a whiff of his aftershave, fresh and inviting, coming with him.

When I fell silent, he said, 'From the statement the nurse made immediately afterward, it happened exactly as you described. Except, she was on edge thanks to what you told her and was more aware of her surroundings than she would usually be when leaving work. She had her keys in her hand and jabbed him in the face when he jumped out at her.'

It almost sounded as if he was thanking me. Brow creased, I said, 'Last night your detective accused me of being behind the attack. Are you saying you think I'm telling the truth, that it really was a vision?'

'Stranger things have happened, especially in this town lately.'

From his voice, I was sure he was smiling.

'What do you mean?'

'I've been called in on a couple of unusual cases, ones

that make me think things like visions could be possible.' Now he sounded rueful. 'Was last night the first time you've had a vision?'

'Yes. It better be the last time too. It's brought me nothing but trouble.'

'It did help save Juanita Daniels.'

I bit my bottom lip. He had a point but while I was happy she'd escaped, I did not want to go through anything like this ever again. I had enough to deal with as it was, without adding nightmarish visions to the mix.

'Has there ever been a sign there was anything unusual about you, before yesterday?' he asked after a long silence. 'No unexplained things happening around you?'

'You mean other than being blinded in a car accident that wasn't my fault?' I shook my head, not sure where he was going with this line of questioning. 'I'm just an ordinary girl. I'm boring.'

'I very much doubt that,' he said, voice deepening even further.

All of a sudden, I remembered I hadn't showered or changed since Mum and Dad had been to see me the day before. God, I must look a mess. I resisted the urge to pat my hair to check if it was sticking up all over the place, relieved when his mobile phone rang.

'This is Constable Carlton,' he said, and then there was silence for a moment before I heard footsteps and the door to my room opening and closing. I could hear him talking on his phone as he paced up and down the hall outside my room, his deep voice pitched low.

I remained in the same position, not sure what to do now.

When he returned he said, 'I'm sorry, I have to go. Thank you for talking to me about your vision. Here's my card in case you think there is anything else I should know. I'm placing it on the bedside table.'

Moments later he left, and I leaned back into the pillow, wondering what else this day was going to bring.

3

Later that morning, after I'd managed to shower and change into a button up shirt and a pair of shorts, the door swung open and a familiar voice said, 'And how are you feeling today, Belinda?'

'I'll be better when you send me home, Dr Phillips.'

'Well, let's have a look at you and we might be able to make that happen.'

'Really? I can go home?' I eagerly turned my head toward his voice.

'Now, now, it can't be that bad. Nurse, if you could assist me?'

A firm hand touched my shoulder and I lay back. The silent nurse undid the buttons of my shirt to show the doctor the healing wounds. I stifled a wince at the cool touch, wondering if this was the same nurse who had destroyed my flowers.

The doctor probed my ribs and I held back another wince. I needed to get out of there and didn't want the doctor to think I was in too much pain to be discharged. The nurse redid my buttons and then held my head still as the doctor went through the familiar routine of checking my eyes for any sign of improvement.

My optimism took a dip when there was no change, not that I'd expected any given the constant darkness that enveloped me.

'Dr Phillips, do you think there's any chance my eyesight will return on its own?' I'd asked previously, but had never been given a straight answer.

Dr Phillips sighed. 'The corneal lacerations have healed well, but that is not the case with the damage to your optic nerves. Unfortunately, that is one area of the eye we can not fix. It is possible they will continue to heal over time and you may regain some of your sight, but at this stage it's not looking likely.'

Tears pricked my eyes and I dashed them away, giving a quick nod.

After a moment of silence, he continued in an overly jovial voice. 'Well then, let's check how your lungs are working.'

He asked me to breathe in deeply before exhaling as much air as I could.

'How did that feel? Any pain or discomfort. Any breathlessness?'

'No, it felt fine.' I didn't even have to lie.

'You'll need to come back in a week so the ophthalmologist can check your eyes, and continue your meetings with the psychologists and occupational therapists, but you're ready to go home.'

'Thank you, Dr Phillips.' I leaned back against the pillows as I heard him leave the room, thankful one thing had gone my way today.

'What are you smiling for?'

I stiffened. It was the nurse from earlier.

'Bet you think you're real clever. But—'

'Belinda, honey,' Mum called out as she entered the room. 'We just met Dr Phillips in the hall. He said you can come home. Isn't that great?'

'Yeah, it's great, Mum. Let's get out of here.'

'I'll get started on the discharge paperwork,' said the nurse.

She left the room and I pushed all thought of her out of my mind while Mum packed my things into the small suitcase stashed in the bottom of the wardrobe. I slid off the bed and waited for her to put shoes near my feet.

'I hear you're ready to blow this joint,' said Dad as he entered the room.

Slipping my feet into my shoes, I smiled in the direction of his voice. 'Yeah, and it's about time too.'

'Hey, it can't have been that bad.'

'You have no idea.'

'Well, you're getting out of here now and with what happened last night I'll be glad you're safe at home,' said Dad.

'What happened last night?'

Mum's voice was accompanied by the sound of zipping as she closed the suitcase.

'Two of the nurses were attacked in the carpark. They caught the guy but it just goes to show you can't be too careful these days,' he said.

'Belinda, is that why you have a card from a police officer? I found it on your bedside table.'

Careful to keep my face blank, not wanting to discuss my vision, I said, 'The police questioned me about the attack last night, and again this morning. Constable Carlton left his card in case I remembered anything else. No big deal.'

'But you're blind. How could you be a witness?' Mum asked.

The silence that greeted this statement had the power to deafen.

'I mean—'

'I know what you meant, Mum. One of my nurses was the first to be attacked.'

'Well, I'm glad they caught the man responsible.'

'Me too.'

I waited for one of them to take my arm to lead me from the room, resisting the urge to put my free hand out in front of me to make sure I wasn't going to bang into everything. This was going to be what my life was like from now on, having to rely on other people to help me with even simple tasks until I was able to manage on my own.

But at least I was going home, away from the hospital staff who hated me. Not that I'd lived with Mum and Dad for the last six months. I'd been sharing a flat with my cousin, Grace. Still, after nineteen years roaming around the house I'd grown up in, I was sure I'd have no problems navigating my way around even though I wouldn't be able to see where I was going.

My rare good mood had Mum and Dad smiling as they finalised my paperwork and led me to the car. I could hear it in their voices. It did feel strange though, sitting in the backseat and not being able to look out the windows and see where we were going. I closed my eyes and let the excited chatter of my parents wash over me.

'Everyone is going to be thrilled when they hear you're home. We've had so many people asking when you were getting out so they can come and visit,' said Mum.

My good mood fled. In the hospital I had been able to control who came, making it clear to the nursing staff that I did not want a constant stream of visitors. At home I would be at the mercy of Mum and Dad, who from the sounds of it were planning a welcome home party.

'I'd really like to wait a while, before I start seeing people,' I said.

'Oh, are you sure?' Mum asked, tone subdued.

'Just give me a few days to settle in. It's a lot to get used to.'

'Okay, if that's what you want. They'll be disappointed, but I'm sure they'll understand. We'll see if Grace can make it over for tea tonight, though. She's been missing you like crazy, so we've had her over for dinner a couple of times a week.'

Grace had visited me almost every day, and while she hadn't said anything I knew she'd have to find a new flatmate to help cover the rent now I had no way of paying my share. The occupational therapist from the hospital had said I'd be able to go back to my part time job at the bakery soon, but how was I supposed to serve customers if I couldn't see what I was doing?

Until I was able to manage on my own, I would have to rely on Mum and Dad to take care of me physically and financially. I'd worked so hard to be independent, and now I was back where I'd started when I finished high school last year.

It wasn't fair for me to lose my eyesight because a motorist had been speeding and lost control as he rounded a corner. Yet he walked away from the accident with a few broken ribs, while I had my entire future destroyed.

I wanted to go back in time.

I wanted my eyesight back.

'Belle, honey, we're home,' said Dad.

Sitting up straight, I wiped my eyes as the car slowed down ready to turn into the driveway. It came to a stop and I could hear clanking and squeaking as the roller door on the garage began to rise.

Coolness enveloped me as the car moved into the garage and Dad turned off the engine. I unbuckled the seat belt, climbing out of the car and heading for the door connecting the garage with the house. Working from memory and steadying myself with a hand on the wall, I flushed with a sense of accomplishment when I reached the door.

Standing to the side as Mum unlocked the sliding security screen, I entered the house first and kept one hand on the wall as I slowly made my way toward the lounge. Once I arrived I took a deep breath, inhaling all the familiar scents, and for the first time since I'd woken up and realised I was blind I felt at peace.

'Have a seat, honey, and I'll fix you something to eat,' said Mum, followed by footsteps heading toward the kitchen.

I stretched out a hand until I felt the back of the couch and gratefully slumped into the plush cushions, rubbing my hands over the soft suede on either side of me. I rested my head back and closed my eyes, revelling in the luxurious comfort of the well-padded couch, so unlike the hard chair that had been placed in front of the window in the corner of the hospital room.

Mum quickly returned with a plate of cheese and tomato on crackers, the salt and pepper sprinkled liberally over them stinging my lips.

'Now, I know you've just got home but we need to think about your schedule. They said it's important to get into a routine as soon as possible,' said Mum.

'They?'

'The Easton Community Centre. They gave your father and me some pamphlets and there's a CD for you to listen to, telling you what services they offer. We need to set up a weekly appointment with the resident counsellor, Dr O'Hanlon. You'll also want to start Braille lessons as soon as possible and there are other classes that teach you how to navigate an unknown area. There's also a CD on the merits of guide dogs versus using a cane. Have you thought about what you'd be more comfortable with?'

I recoiled. 'I don't want to talk about it.' I'd just got

home. Was it too much to ask for some time to adjust?

'Belinda, the sooner we get you started the better.'

'Better for who?' I leant forward to place the empty plate down on the coffee table but couldn't find it.

'Oh, we moved the coffee table to the side of the room so you wouldn't bang into it,' said Mum.

I froze, feeling like an idiot waving my plate in the air. 'That's just great. Why not rearrange the whole house while you're at it so I'll have absolutely no idea where anything is.'

There was silence.

'You moved more than the coffee table, didn't you?'

'We wanted to make it easy for you to get around, so we moved a few things. There's no need to get upset.'

'Mum, this was the one place I was sure I'd be okay. But now you've changed it all around.'

'I'm sorry, honey. We'll change it back, if that's what you want.'

I shook my head, standing, still holding the plate clutched in tight fingers. I started walking toward the kitchen, moving slowly, with my free hand out in front of me.

'I'll take that.'

'No thanks, I can do it myself.'

I continued walking until I reached the wall and entered the dining area. The kitchen was on the other side and I felt my way to the sink, placing the plate on the bench. Next I turned with my arm outstretched in front of me and searched for the connecting door to the hallway.

Mum was quiet, but I could hear her breathing as she followed every step I made.

'I want to go to my room and figure out where everything is. You don't need to hover.'

'Okay, honey. Give me a yell if you need me.'

I didn't answer, busy concentrating on where I was going.

Despite my early optimism I was finding it harder to navigate through the house than I'd thought. I had to rely on memory, but all my life I'd taken sight for granted. While I knew the layout of the house, some of the details escaped me. I'd need to focus on each room until I'd got them sorted in my head.

Once I reached the hallway I tried to remember how far it was to my old room. Trailing my fingers along the wall, I felt the gap for the laundry door. Next would be the bathroom and toilet. My room was opposite the toilet and I stretched out a hand until I reached the door.

It was open. I stepped inside the cool room and closed the door behind me. Then I leant up against the hard wood and contemplated the space I had spent much of my life in, wondering how it could have become so strange to me in a short period of time.

I took a step forward, and then another, until my legs pressed up against the bed and I resisted the urge to throw myself down on the soft bedspread, to curl up and cry. Instead, I set about familiarising myself with the room, letting the smell of it wrap around me, glad to be out of the sterile hospital environment.

Mum and Grace had collected my clothes from the flat earlier in the week and said they'd done their best to arrange them in the same manner as I'd had them, to make it easier for me to find things. I felt my way to the dresser, opening each drawer to check the contents. Then I started on the bedside tables before tackling the wardrobe.

Once I'd finished my inspection of the room I sank onto the bed and curled into a ball.

All my clothes were here, my toiletries, even many of the knick knacks I'd collected over the years, but none of my art supplies. It stung, that they had been left at the flat, but I had to face the truth behind Mum's decision not to bring them.

I was blind.
That part of my life was over.
But I had no idea who I was if I wasn't an artist.

4

I had no idea how long I'd been asleep. My dreams had been dark and confusing, filling me with dread as a faceless man pursued me through a dark landscape. Desperate to escape, not knowing who he was or why he was chasing me, I'd wrenched myself awake, heart pounding. I let it settle before I swung my legs over the side of the bed and stood up.

My legs collapsed under me as a riot of colour and noise assaulted my mind. It was as though a dozen people were talking at once and I clasped my hands over my ears in an attempt to block it out. The noise barged through my defences as the image that accompanied it crystallized.

I had a side-on view of a bus filled with older men and women. They were chatting loudly, smiling and animated. A sign on the side of the bus read 'Lakeview Retirement Village'. The rumble of the bus's engine was accompanied by the scraping of tyres on the bitumen road. From the colour of the sky I guessed it to be late afternoon and some of the residents had been on an outing and were now on their way home.

The vision shifted focus to the interior of the bus. The driver, unlike his passengers, was quiet as he navigated the large bus around the manmade lake that gave the retirement village its name, heading for the bridge that would take him over to the other side. He looked to be around the same age as many of the retirees in his care, with a bald head and incongruously bushy eyebrows. Under the eyebrows his pale blue eyes were rimmed in red. One hand left the steering wheel to rub at his arm and he winced.

As I was forced to watch on, his eyes went wide.

He swayed in the seat, face grey as he clutched his chest. He slumped over the steering wheel, foot still pressing down on the accelerator. Bereft of guidance, the large vehicle missed the turn onto the bridge, instead heading for the embankment. Within seconds the bus left the road and became airborne until the weight drove it nose down into the lake.

The retirees inside the bus screamed as they were flung forward in their seats. They scrambled over each other, fighting to get to the rear doors as water lapped the windows at the front of the bus. One elderly gentleman went against the flow of people to aid the driver and lost his footing, falling backward, head hitting the floor with a loud thud. He slid to the front of the bus and lay motionless. Water seeped into the bus through gaps in the seal around the front doors, filling the stairwell, lapping at the feet of the unconscious man.

At the rear of the bus, gripping the backs of the seats to stop themselves from sliding, the retirees cried out and urged the ones in front to get the back doors open. Finally someone found the emergency release button and the doors opened with a whoosh. A bottleneck formed in the doorway as they all attempted to escape the sinking bus at once.

More water poured into the bus from the front. The unconscious man on the floor was covered up to his knees, upper body out of the water for now. The bus driver wasn't so lucky.

Still slumped over the steering wheel, with water rapidly filling the space beneath him, his head was about to go under. His laboured breathing made bubbles as the water slowly but surely crept up to engulf him. As his lungs filled with water his body jerked, the seatbelt holding him in place until the violent movements ceased.

The weight of the water drove the bus further into the lake and it consumed the unconscious man on the floor.

At the rear only a few passengers had managed to escape the sinking bus, the more sprightly retirees fighting their way through the door and setting out for the bank. Two gentlemen had stayed behind to help those less agile, but they were hampered by the water continuing to flood in.

Water streamed through the open doorway as the bus lost its battle to stay afloat. One more retiree managed to struggle out through the inrushing water before the bus was completely engulfed and sank to rest on the lake bottom. He trod water, then was suddenly wrenched under. He reappeared moments later with a woman in his arms. She'd managed to grab his ankle to pull herself out of the bus. She sagged in his arms, all her energy spent, and he slowly dragged her to shore.

The vision released me with a snap and my head recoiled, hitting the bedside table behind me. Shaking off the pain, I struggled to my feet and stumbled for the door. I had to tell the police what I'd seen. They had to stop the bus.

I found the door handle and wrenched it open.

'Mum, Dad,' I called out, tears filling my eyes as I relived the horrible vision. So many people dead.

'Belinda, honey, what's wrong?' Mum's arms wrapped around me.

I clutched at her. 'What time is it?'

'It's a little after three. You slept through lunch. Do you want something to eat?'

I shook my head. If the timing in the vision was right, the accident would happen within hours. I had to stop it from coming true.

'Where's the card for Constable Carlton? There's going to be a bus crash. I need to warn him or people are going to die.'

I started to shake.

'Belinda, you're not making any sense.' She took hold of my shoulders. 'You need to calm down.'

'I saw a bus crash in the lake. The one from that new retirement village. The driver is going to have a heart attack.'

'You saw it? I don't understand. Did you have a nightmare?'

'No, it was a vision. Like the one yesterday when I saw my nurse getting attacked. That's why the police came to see me.'

'What's going on? What's wrong?'

Dad placed a hand on my back and I turned toward him, desperate to get someone to understand.

'She had a nightmare,' said Mum.

'It wasn't a nightmare. It was a vision and it's going to come true if I don't warn them. I need to talk to Constable Carlton now, please. You need to ring him for me.'

'Come on, Belle, why don't you have a seat and we'll talk about it.'

Dad pulled me out of Mum's arms and steered me toward the lounge room.

'There's nothing to talk about. People are going to die.' Frustration ate away at me, bile rising in my throat as I fought to stay calm.

They didn't believe me. They weren't going to ring the police. I'd have to do it myself. Shaking off Dad's hand, I felt my way to the kitchen, banging against the walls and doorjamb in my haste.

I took no notice of the pain, focused on my goal.

Sweeping an arm across the bench, I found the phone cradle and picked up the handset, trying to remember where the buttons were. '0' was always in the middle at the bottom. I quickly pressed it three times and waited for the emergency operator to answer.

'I need the police. I have to talk to Constable Scott Carlton. He's at the Easton Police Station.'

'Is this an emergency? This line is for emergencies only.'

'Yes, it's an emergency. People are going to die if you don't put me through to him. There's going to be a bus crash and he needs to stop it.'

I knew I sounded crazy, but the whole situation was insane. Normal people did not have visions. What was wrong with me?

'Belle, give me the phone.'

Dad put his hand on my shoulder, trying to turn me to face him.

I pulled out of his grasp and hunched over the phone to make sure he couldn't take it from me, keeping my back to him and Mum. Breathless, I waited for the constable to answer. Mum and Dad kept urging me to hang up but I tuned them out, clutching the phone as hard as I could.

'Constable Carlton.'

Relief surged through me at the sound of his voice and I took a moment to gather my wits. I had to make him believe me. I couldn't sound like a crazy person.

'This is Belinda Gregory. I had another vision. A bus from a retirement village, the one at Lakeview Estate, is going to crash into the lake. The driver is going to have a heart attack and most of the passengers drown. You have to stop it.' I spoke in a rush, needing to get it all out before he stopped me.

A long silence met my words, and I held my breath.

Finally, when my nerves were about to snap, he asked, 'Are you sure?'

'Do you really think I'd be ringing you if I wasn't? It's not as if I wanted to have another vision. You have to hurry. It is going to happen this afternoon.'

I didn't have an exact time, and there'd been no indication of the date in my visit, but it felt right to say it would happen today.

'Relax, I believe you,' he said. 'I'm just going to need something more to convince Detective Johnson. Where are you? I'll come to you.'

'Thank you,' I said, sagging against the counter. 'I'm at my parents' house.'

I gave him the address and then hung up the phone, head reeling.

Dad scooped me up in his arms and soon I was sitting on the couch with a cup of tea that tasted as though it had at least five spoons of sugar in it, Mum's cure-all for shock. The sugar hit my system with a jolt and I revived but brushed aside their questions.

'I'll explain more when the police get here.'

I knew they were worried, but hoped they'd understand when they heard the whole story.

Constable Carlton arrived five minutes later, but to my dismay he had brought Detective Johnson with him. I could sense him looming over me as I described the horrific vision of the bus going into the lake, stressing the need for him to hurry up and prevent it happening.

Detective Johnson was the first to break the silence after I finished talking.

'You expect us to believe that rubbish?'

'How can you say that? After what happened yesterday, why don't you believe me?'

'I can't prove it, but I still think you're behind the attack on both nurses and made up a story about having visions to cover your tracks.'

'Belinda would never do something like that,' said Mum.

'Making a hoax call is a serious offence and a waste of my time,' said Johnson. 'You can be assured I will charge your daughter when this vision is shown to be bogus.'

'Detective Johnson, with all due respect,' said Dad, 'it's clear my daughter experienced a terrible nightmare, one so vivid she was sure it was real or she would never have called the police. Surely you can't blame her for that?'

Much as I appreciated Dad sticking up for me, I needed them all to know I was telling the truth.

Sucking in air, I had another attempt at making them listen. If that didn't work I would call a taxi to take me to the lake so I could stand in front of the bus to make it stop.

'It wasn't a nightmare. I was awake. That bus is going to crash and people are going to die. It's going to happen soon and none of you is doing anything about it.'

'Are you sure about the time?'

I turned toward Constable Carlton, reassured by the matter of fact tone he used. 'From the position of the sun and the shadows on the road I'd say the accident takes place a little before five o'clock.'

Johnson gave a bitter laugh. 'Position of the sun... You really expect me to believe you can tell the time from that and some shadows?'

'Yes, Detective Johnson, I do. I'm an artist and details are everything to me.' I snapped out the words, frustrated beyond belief with his obstinate refusal to consider I was telling the truth.

'It's half-past four now. Maybe we could swing by the lake on the way back to the station,' said Constable Carlton. 'It wouldn't hurt to take a look.'

When Detective Johnson grudgingly agreed, tears pricked my eyes. I turned my head in the direction I thought Constable Carlton was. 'Thank you. Thank you so much.'

They quickly left, Mum and Dad escorting them out while I remained on the couch, lost in the dark, wringing my hands. I hated waiting.

Mum and Dad came back into the lounge but they didn't say anything. They probably didn't know what to say. Still, I could feel them looking at me.

Finally, Mum gave a sigh. 'I guess I'd better get dinner started. Grace will be here soon, if she can get out of work on time.'

I lay on the couch and closed my eyes. Straight away, images from my vision assailed me and I sat up, drawing my knees to my chest and wrapping my arms around them. I wouldn't be able to rest until I knew those people on the bus were safe.

'Hey, you doing okay?'

The couch dipped as Dad lowered his large frame down and placed an arm around my shoulders.

I leaned into his comforting bulk. 'No, I'm not okay.'

'It'll get better. You'll see. We'll get through this.'

'I guess it can't get any worse,' I said, hoping it was true.

5

A knock at the door came at six o'clock.

Mum hurried to open it and I heaved a sigh when I heard a familiar voice.

'Hey, Belle. Glad to see they let you out of that place. Hospitals suck.'

'Grace, you work in a vet surgery. How can you hate hospitals?' Mum asked. 'And how come you're so early? I didn't expect you until around seven. Dinner won't be ready until then.'

'A vet surgery is nothing like a hospital. We get cute and cuddly animals. They get sick and cranky people. And I got an early mark for once. Andrew got back from his holiday a day early and sent me home. He took pity on me after he heard how many hours I've been doing with Penny off sick and everything.'

I knew I was the "everything" Grace was referring too. She would never come out and say it though. Her attitude about hospitals extended to anyone who was sick. She might have oodles of empathy for those cute and cuddly animals but Grace had never had any patience for humans who were ill.

'So, what's new with you?' This was accompanied by the sound of Grace sinking into the lounge chair opposite the couch. 'Something's got Aunt Laura in a tizz.'

'Guess she's not used to having a freak for a daughter.'

'Belle, being blind doesn't make you a freak.'

'That wasn't what I was talking about.'

Another knock came at the door and I listened as Grace

got up to open it. She returned a minute later.

'Ah, Belle, there're two very wet police officers here to see you.'

My heart stopped beating then started again in a rush and it was all I could hear as Mum bustled around grabbing towels for Detective Johnson and Constable Carlton to dry themselves.

'Is everyone okay?' I asked.

'We arrived on scene just as the bus veered off the road and into the lake,' said Constable Carlton. 'But we were able to get all the passengers off before it sank.'

I sagged back, relief leaving me dizzy.

'I'll take it from here,' said Detective Johnson, his voice tense.

What followed was a gruelling interrogation as Johnson tried to trick me into revealing some conspiracy. Despite being told by the ambulance officers on scene it appeared as if the bus driver had a heart attack, with the retirees who had been sitting behind him verifying this diagnosis, he was still trying to pin it on me. He didn't want to believe the alternative.

I wished I didn't have to believe it either. But I didn't have that luxury.

After I could offer no further explanation to satisfy Johnson, he and the constable finally left and I sat down to dinner with my family.

I brushed aside Mum's offer to cut my food into bite-sized pieces, smarting at being treated like a child in front of Grace. Lovely, vivacious, Grace with her black hair, smoky grey eyes, and flawless complexion, who I'd heard flirting with Constable Carlton while Detective Johnson had been questioning me. She'd been all over the guy, going on and on about how he had saved all those people in the bus and what a hero he was. With the detective keen to prove I was a fake, I'd been unable to hear the constable's quiet responses.

During dinner Grace kept the conversation going with a story about how she had helped save a litter of puppies when they had become stuck while being born. I was grateful for her, as she kept Mum and Dad from focusing on what had happened as I struggled to eat dinner without making a mess of myself.

I couldn't continue like this. I needed help managing my condition.

'I want to go to the Community Centre tomorrow. Mum, can you take me?' I asked when Grace stopped talking to take a breath.

'Of course, honey. I'm so glad you've decided to check it out. They have some wonderful programs.'

Grace once again began talking about what had happened that day at work as she cleared the table around me. I finally finished off my meal and sat back.

'Belle, if you've finished your dinner you can go help Grace with the dishes,' said Dad.

'But I'm blind.'

'So? Doesn't mean you can't wield a tea towel. Get to it.'

A smile bloomed on my face, despite having to take on a chore I normally hated. I carefully made my way to the kitchen and took the tea towel Mum handed me. The dirty dishes were piled up on the bench to the left of the sink and got placed in the draining rack on the right. I gingerly picked up a plate out of the rack and wiped it with the tea towel before placing it on the bench to be put away later.

Beside me, Grace scrubbed the dishes clean in the sink and piled them up in the draining rack. 'Hurry up, slacko. I'm running out of room.'

'I'm going as fast as I can. Give me a break.'

'Sure, if you answer me one question. Do you know if that constable has a girlfriend?'

'Oh my God, I was right. You were flirting with him.'

'Of course I was. He was seriously cute. Tall, blue eyes, and a chiselled jaw. The guy could be a model or an actor with his looks.'

While it was good to be able to picture a face to go with his deep voice, it didn't feel right to have Grace mooning over Constable Carlton.

'Haven't you girls finished those dishes yet? Your mother is waiting for her cuppa.'

'Nearly done, Uncle John,' said Grace.

Glad we were off the topic of Constable Carlton, I was happy to spend the rest of the evening sitting in the lounge sipping hot drinks. Despite the nap earlier in the day I was still tired and headed to my room soon after Grace left.

It took a long time for me to fall asleep, even tired as I was, worried another vision would hit. While my sleep was vision free, it was full of nightmares where I wandered lost and alone under a full moon, trying to hide from a faceless man.

My eyes were gritty, thoughts sluggish as Mum drove me to the Community Centre the next day. As soon as we arrived she was whisked away to fill out paperwork, while a girl named Karen offered to give me a tour.

'You'll like it here,' she said. 'There's so much to do and the centre is very interactive so we encourage our members to participate as much as they want to.'

'Sounds like fun. I can hardly wait,' I lied.

'Belinda, I know it doesn't feel like it could possibly happen but it will get better.'

'That's easy for you to say. You're not the one who can't see.'

'Maybe not, but I've seen lots of people like you come through the centre and once they have accepted the changes they have all gone on to lead fulfilling lives. You can too, if you set your mind to it.'

Karen let me stew for a while before talking again.

'Your mother tells me you're an artist. We could use someone like you around here to brighten up the place.'

'I was an artist. I'll have to find another career now, one that doesn't require eyes.'

'You're still an artist, Belinda. Losing your eyesight doesn't change that. You've just got to figure out a new way to express your talent. Don't worry, we can help you with that.'

I wanted to tell Karen how ridiculous her statement was, but someone called out for her. She led me over to a couch saying she'd be back in a minute, and then came the sound of more people entering the lounge area, though it sounded as though they were on the other side of the room.

'Karen is right,' someone said, making me jump. I hadn't realised anyone was sitting beside me.

'You think being blind is the end of the world,' she said, 'but soon you will realise you've been given a gift.'

A hand touched my arm and I pulled away. I did not need random strangers giving me pep talks.

'Angel,' said a new voice, 'Dr O'Hanlon is ready to see you now.'

The person sitting beside me got up, and said, 'I'll see you tomorrow, Belinda. I can't wait to get to know you better.'

Angel left and I heard the sound of more people entering the room.

I leaned into the couch and closed my eyes, to make it look as if I was resting, not wanting any of them to come and talk to me.

The vision began the second my eyes closed.

I was looking at a large building and recognised it instantly. It was one of the warehouses near the CBD that had been turned into an apartment block a few years back. One of my friends from university had rented a bottom floor apartment for a while before she'd moved with a couple of other girls to a house with a backyard and a pool.

Stacey had never felt safe in the ground floor apartment as the building hadn't been renovated very well. The power was always going out due to faulty wiring and the walls would shake when a door was slammed in neighbouring apartments. She'd been worried the whole place was going to fall down while she slept.

In the vision, the building looked quiet, peaceful. It was dark, the streetlights casting shadows on the front door. With a gasp, I realised not all the shadows were cast by the light.

These shadows were moving, wreathing their way out of the windows of an apartment on the second floor. They began to pour out in a thick stream and behind them I could see a flickering orange light even as the shadows appeared in other windows.

The apartment was on fire.

The fire quickly spread from room to room. People could be seen battering frantically at the windows, caught behind security screens, their hysterical screams lost to the night.

Caught unawares, those in the ground floor apartments were woken by the commotion above them and fled the building in their pyjamas. Some had mobile phones in hand and dialled for help, unable to do anything for the tenants still trapped in the burning apartment block.

Sirens filled the air. Fire engines came to a screeching halt outside the building and quickly went to work. Firemen entered the building via the front door but soon exited. The stairs were engulfed in flames. There was no way to get upstairs to free those trapped on the upper floors.

The firemen scaled ladders, prying security screens lose and gaining entry to the building, managing to free several of the trapped inhabitants. But the fire was too hot, vast and unmanageable. Eventually it became too dangerous for the firemen and they had to withdraw. Some people were still trapped in their apartments. Soon their cries could no longer be heard.

A few residents managed to make it to the roof and the firemen refocused their efforts, trying to get to them before the fire did. Two more people were rescued, while one man fell to his death after launching himself at the ladder before it got close enough, fire licking at his heels.

I cried out when the vision released me from its grasp. I shot up from the couch, frantically shaking my head, trying to clear the horrific images. That man's crumpled body on the sidewalk, the dull thud as it connected with the concrete, abruptly cutting off his despairing scream.

'Belinda, what's wrong?'

I sagged into Mum's arms, grateful she had returned. 'I had another vision. There's going to be a fire. I have to tell the police.'

This time Mum did not argue. She whipped out her mobile phone and dialled the number for Constable Carlton, passing the phone into my hands when he answered.

Gripping the phone tightly, I told him what I'd seen.

'Okay, I'll check it out and call you back. Are you at home?'

'No, I'm at the Community Centre with Mum.'

'Go home and wait for me to call. And, Belinda, don't tell anyone what you saw. We don't want to start a panic.'

149

'Okay.' I handed the phone back to Mum and waited as she explained to Karen that we had a family emergency and had to cut the tour short.

Once we got home, Mum made another one of her famous sweet, hot teas. I jumped when the phone rang, nearly spilling my tea.

'I'm sorry for taking so long to get back to you,' said Constable Carlton, after Mum handed me the phone. 'We've hit a snag. I want to evacuate the building you saw in your vision, but without actual proof something is going to happen Detective Johnson says we don't have legal grounds to act.'

'But that's crazy. You know my visions come true.'

'I know, and that's why I'm going to check it out after my shift finishes this afternoon. I'll take care of it, okay?'

'Okay. Thanks for calling, Constable Carlton.'

'Please, call me Scott.' His deep voice was firm, sure, filling me with confidence. He would save the people in the building, just as he saved the ones on the bus.

'What do we do now?' Mum asked after I'd hung up the phone.

'We wait and hope Scott is able to stop the fire from happening.' Only, as the hours inched by, I wasn't just worried about the people who lived in the apartment block; now I was worried about him.

He was going to be on the scene, trying to stop the fire from happening. But what if he didn't? What if something went wrong and he got hurt?

Or worse?

6

The nightmare started with me running through the moonlit night, once more pursued by the faceless man, the long white dress I was wearing tangling on branches and slowing me down. Only this time he was calling my name, saying it over and over again. Saying I couldn't get away from him now he knew who I was.

As before, I knew it was a nightmare and not a vision, but it felt so real I was sure if he caught me I would never be free. Even the realisation that I could see in the nightmare was no comfort to me.

Loud banging finally pulled me from sleep and I groggily sat up. My head felt like it was stuffed with cottonwool and I sat on the edge of the bed until I felt able to stand without falling over. Even then my steps were wobbly as I made my way to the bedroom door and stepped into the hall.

I heard a commotion at the front door; Dad arguing with someone.

'Belinda Gregory, can you tell us about your vision?'

'Get out of my house,' said Dad, voice tense. 'Belle, go into the lounge. I'll take care of this.'

I retreated and sat on the couch, questions blowing away the cottonwool clouding my head. Had my vision come true? Did the apartment building burn down? Was Constable Carlton, Scott, okay?

'Belinda, honey, drink this. It will make you feel better.'

Mum placed a cup in my hand and to my surprise it was hot chocolate instead of tea. Still, it was hot and sweet.

'What did you give me?'

Mum had urged me to try some of her headache tablets after dinner, when my head had been thumping. I'd taken two and became sleepy almost straight away, despite being sure I'd never be able to rest while waiting for news about the fire. Mum had helped me to bed and I'd crashed the moment my head hit the pillow.

'Just a mild sedative. Dr Phillips said there might be times when you'd have trouble sleeping and I thought this would be a good time to use them. You wouldn't have got any sleep otherwise.'

'You drugged me?'

'It was for your own good. You needed your rest.'

While I knew Mum thought she'd done the right thing, if I couldn't trust my own mother how was I going to learn to trust complete strangers in the outside world? Maybe I should just hide in my bedroom and never come out.

Dad finally managed to get the door closed on the nosy reporter who had woken us all up.

'Laura, close the curtains,' he said as he walked into the lounge. 'He's got a blasted cameraman with him. I'm going to ring Dave and let him know I need more time off.'

Gratitude washed through me, knowing he was going to stay home from work. The thought of being trapped inside the house, with just Mum to fend off the nosy reporter, made me shudder. Although I was sure she would do whatever it took to protect me.

The phone rang, making me jump.

I tensed as Mum answered it. 'Hello?'

'No comment.' Mum slammed the phone back on the base only to have it ring a second later. It rang out, only to begin again.

'Unplug it,' said Dad when he returned to the lounge.

While the silence that followed was welcome, the knowledge a reporter was camped outside had me jumping at the slightest sound. I put the hot chocolate on the coffee table, not trusting myself to hold it steady. I'd just placed it down when a loud knock shook the front door.

'This is Constable Carlton.'

Dad hurried to open the door and I smelled smoke as Scott approached me.

'Is everyone okay? Did you save them?' I gripped the bottom of my pyjama top, scrunching it, wishing I'd thought to get changed.

'Yes, Belinda. I was able to get everyone out of the building before the fire took hold,' he said, his tone curiously flat.

'Thank God. I was so worried.' I smiled, tears welling in my eyes.

'Is that why you called the reporter and tipped him off? Because you were worried your story wouldn't make front page news tomorrow?'

'What are you talking about?' I dashed my tears away, taken aback by the coolness in his voice, so unlike our previous conversations. 'I only told you.'

'Then how did he know?'

'I don't know, but it wasn't from me.' I stood, refusing to sit there and let him look down on me. But I misjudged the distance and banged into him, rebounding off his hard chest. I stumbled backward, and would have fallen if he had not wrapped his arms around me.

Locked in darkness, I had no way of knowing if I was glaring in the right direction but gave it a good shot, feeling his grip tighten.

'Could it have been someone from the Community Centre?' Dad asked.

At the reasonable suggestion Scott relaxed his grip, although he didn't let go.

'Ten people could have been standing next to me and I wouldn't have noticed. Mum, did you see anyone?'

'I was more worried about you than checking to see if anyone was listening in on our conversation. But there were people in the room with us. Any one of them could have eavesdropped.'

'It could have been anybody who tipped that reporter off.' I frowned up at Scott, conscious of the warmth of his hands on my back.

My palms were pressed against the hard planes of his chest. Cheeks flushing with heat, I pushed against him and he let me go. I flopped down on the couch, and listened as he backed away. But even though he had moved over to the other side of the room I could still feel him watching me.

'What I want to know is what happens now? That reporter knows Belinda has visions. Can you get him to go away?' Mum asked.

'Unfortunately, no. With luck, though, if you don't give him anything more to go on, and stick with "No Comment", he'll get bored and leave of his own accord. In the meantime, I'll be looking into just how the story got leaked.'

I stiffened, sure he still didn't believe I had nothing to do with it, as if I was after my fifteen minutes of fame. He'd been convinced I'd gone to the press, and yet he'd stopped me from falling. His arms had wrapped around me without hesitation, his large hands holding me steady. I remembered the feel of his chest beneath my palms, and blushed as the thought of what it would be like to touch him without the shirt in the way flashed across my brain.

It was Grace's fault, saying he was cute. My cousin could have him.

After he left, Mum urged me to go back to bed, tucking me in as she used to when I was a child. Now that I knew the people in the apartment block had been saved, and I'd slept off the worst of the sedative, I hoped the rest of the night would be dream free. But the nightmare started almost as soon as I drifted off. This time I got the impression there was someone else behind the faceless man, a shadowy figure calling the shots.

The shadow whispered in the ear of the faceless man, urging him to violence against me, avarice in his half-heard tone as he promised a bonus on my capture. I kept running, with no idea where the dark road was taking me, desperate to get away from them both.

The next morning, I sat at the dining table and struggled to eat a piece of toast, conscious of the reporter still waiting outside. Every now and then he would knock on the front door and call out to me, and my body would tense up. Finally I gave up on eating and made my way to the lounge room where Mum and Dad were conversing in low tones while watching one of the morning shows. A salesman was on, talking about a new cooking appliance that he promised would revolutionise any kitchen, and I managed a smile at the mention of a set of free steak knives. No matter what else was going on in the world, some things never changed.

I took a seat on the couch, rubbing my temples.

'Are you okay, Belle?' Dad asked.

'Nothing a new set of eyes wouldn't fix,' I said, a wry smile curving my lips.

Before he could respond, Easton was mentioned on the television.

'We're crossing live to Josh Holbert who is in Easton right now. Josh, is it true what we're hearing, that Belinda Gregory has had more than one vision?'

'Yes, Lisa, that is correct. My sources tell me Miss Gregory has had three visions of horrible events that have all come true in the last few days. As I told you earlier, Belinda was blinded in a car accident two weeks ago, but while she may have lost her sight, it seems she gained the ability to see into the future.'

'Turn it off.' I shot to my feet, hands over my ears. 'I don't want to hear any more.'

The television went silent, but I knew the damage was already done.

Mum's mobile phone rang and after a moment's hesitation she answered it. They still hadn't reconnected the home phone from the night before but they knew it was only a matter of time before the media found the mobile numbers.

'Grace, you scared the life out of me. I thought you were a reporter. Yes, Belinda's here. Hang on, I'll give her the phone.'

I held the phone, wincing when Grace's excited voice boomed in my ear. 'You're all over the news. I can't believe you didn't tell me you had another vision.'

'We've been kind of busy and the police told me not to tell anyone.'

'I'm sure Constable Carlton didn't mean you couldn't tell me. I am your cousin, after all. He would want me to know what was going on.'

Grace's voice purred when she talked about the detective.

I rolled my eyes. 'You can take that up with him next time you see him.'

'You should hear what people are saying about you on the radio, and they're advertising a special report on the local news tonight.'

'About me?'

'You're a blind girl who has visions. So far half the calls

to the radio station are split down the middle. Half think you're faking it and the other half want to know if you can contact Elvis or Michael Jackson. I wanted to call in and give them a piece of my mind, but didn't want to make the situation worse for you.'

'Thanks,' I said, summoning up a wan smile. 'It's the thought that counts, I guess.'

'Hey, I know it sucks to be going through all this, but at least you have that handsome cop on your side. Maybe you can have him assigned as your personal bodyguard or something. That would be so romantic.'

Face flushing, I said a hasty goodbye, remembering the feel of Scott's hands on my back, the hard planes of his chest beneath my palms. Having him as my bodyguard would not be a good idea, not that he would want to have anything to do with me if he still thought I was behind the leak to the press.

'Honey, is everything okay?'

'I'm fine, Mum. Grace was just checking up on me. Apparently I'm the hot topic for today on the radio as well.'

The rest of the day passed in a blur. People kept knocking on the door, demanding to speak to me. The reporter was the most persistent, but there were others who wanted to talk to a deceased loved one or to find out if Elvis and Michael Jackson were really dead. One guy even had a loud speaker and asked me to marry him, claiming he was psychic too and that our children would be superheroes.

It also didn't take long for people to find out the mobile numbers for the family so Mum and Dad switched them off.

Mum kept urging me to take a nap, but I didn't want to risk having another nightmare. I'd had enough of them to last a decade, not a fan of the way they felt so real. And I'd never pictured myself running through trees, with only the full moon to light my way, in a dress that would suit a gothic heroine in a ghost story.

In the afternoon I curled up on the couch, under a blanket, wishing there was something I could do to help pass the time. If I could see, I'd be able to draw or even read. Mum put a movie on, but I found it hard to follow the storyline with just dialogue and the soundtrack to go on.

Despite my best intentions, I drifted off to sleep and found myself back in the nightmare, running for my life with no idea who was chasing me or why.

I ran until I could run no more, and then turned to face my pursuer.

No more would I let him torment me while I slept.

But no one was there, just a dark shadow that dissipated into nothing.

A loud knock at the door pulled me from the nightmare and I sat up, rubbing my eyes, wondering what drama I would have to deal with now.

7

Some of my apprehension faded when I heard Scott's voice. Then I remembered what had happened last time he was here. Frowning, I finger combed my hair as Mum rushed to let him in, wondering if he was going to accuse me of going to the media again.

After a brief murmur of conversation with Mum, he said, 'Excuse me, Mrs Gregory, but I need to speak to your daughter. If you wouldn't mind giving us a few moments.'

Mum swiftly exited the room. Soon I could hear her clanging dishes together in the kitchen, leaving me alone with Scott, struggling not to fidget under the weight of his stare.

'May I sit down?'

'What? Of course. Have a seat.'

I expected him to sit on one of the armchairs opposite the couch but to my surprise he sat next to me. His weight made the couch dip and I slid toward him. Conscious of my reaction the last time he'd touched me I quickly scooted over to avoid banging into him.

'I'm sorry if I'm making you uncomfortable. I'll leave, and you can do this with another officer when they become available.' The couch bounced as he stood up.

With a deep breath, I waved a hand in the air in front of me. 'No, please, I'm fine. I just get nervous when I can't see people even though they're right next to me.'

'I guess I can understand that,' he said as he sat back down and this time I didn't draw away.

The movement of the couch pulled me closer to him, his

leg brushing against mine, and I could feel the warmth of his body. I swallowed, hoping none of the confusion I felt was evident on my face.

We sat in silence for a moment, and then he shifted position. 'I'm sorry about the way I acted last time I was here. You've had a lot to deal with these past few days and I didn't make it any easier, accusing you of going to the press about your visions.'

His apology sounded sincere, making it hard to drum up any residual anger. 'You're a police officer. It's your job to be suspicious.'

'That's no excuse. You deserve better than that.'

He cleared his throat.

'The tip off to the media about your vision of the fire did come from someone who was at the Easton Community Centre when you were there yesterday. I'm sorry I accused you of being responsible.'

'Sorry enough to make the reporter go away?'

'As I said last night, there isn't a lot I can do other than make sure he stays off your property. Sooner or later something else will come up that takes the heat off you and he'll leave of his own accord. Then you can get back to leading a normal life.'

'I'm not sure I know what a normal life is anymore.'

'You're a strong, intelligent, young woman. You'll figure it out.'

I flushed at his compliment, hating that he could see every emotion flitting across my face while I only had his voice to judge his actions by. It was confusing, and I stood to put some distance between us. He moved at the same time and we banged heads.

'Ouch.' I put a hand up to rub the sore spot and the other flailed behind me for the back of the couch.

160

A firm hand gripped mine, steadying me, and I froze.

His hand was warm and large, engulfing mine. His other hand came up to gently rub the bump on my temple.

'Are you okay? Did I hurt you?'

'I'm okay,' I said, rubbing my eyes and stifling a yawn.

'You look tired. You need to take better care of yourself, get more sleep,' he said. 'You've had three visions that have come true in as many days. It makes sense you'll be having more of them. You need to keep up your strength, to help you deal with the fall out.'

More visions. I didn't want more visions. 'Wasn't three enough?'

I must have said it out loud, because he said, 'Your visions are helping people, Belinda, saving lives. That's a good thing.'

For him maybe, but I did not want this to be my life. Unable to see anything but terrifying incidents, trapped in my parents' home to avoid the scrutiny of the media and anyone else who thought they had a right to know about my visions.

I was supposed to be an artist. I had my whole life planned out.

Without a sound, I began to cry.

Strong arms came around me and I allowed myself to be bundled up against his chest, clutching at him as I cried my heart out.

After a long, gut wrenching episode, I ran out of tears but remained where I was, cradled in his embrace. Then I pulled away.

'I'm sorry, I didn't mean to lose control like that.'

'No problem,' he said quietly. 'It's as good a time to lose control as any. Though I may need to pop home and grab a dry shirt before I head back to the station. Getting soaked is coming to be a habit since I met you.'

He gave a low chuckle that had the extraordinary effect of sending shivers down my spine. He was so close, his arm brushing against mine as we stood side by side.

I remembered the feel of his arms around me, comforting and strong and thought about how safe that had made me feel.

'Belinda,' he said, hand stroking my cheek.

'Yes.' I leaned toward him, felt his hand move to my arm, drawing me even closer. I tilted my head back, tongue darting out to moisten my lips.

'This is a bad idea,' he said, his low voice sending shivers all over my body, the gentle puff of his breath on my face setting my heart racing.

His mouth covered mine, tongue delving between my lips even as his arms crushed me to his chest. I moaned, opening myself to him, tasting him, running my hands through his hair and tugging him even closer.

Then the vision hit.

I gasped, body going rigid as Scott lowered me to the couch. He was calling my name, fear in his voice, but I couldn't answer him, frozen by the force of the vision assailing my senses.

A young woman with long dark hair was running, pursued by a man dressed all in black. It was night, the full moon illuminating the scene as she weaved between bushes that snagged her long white dress as she sought to get away. Her back was to me, but it was so much like my nightmare, I was sure I was the woman being chased. But when she glanced over her shoulder to see how far away her pursuer was, I saw she was a stranger, pretty features distorted with terror when she realised he was gaining on her.

She increased her speed, not paying attention to where she was going, tripping over a tree root and tumbling to the ground.

He was on her before she could scramble back to her feet, wrenching hold of her arm and spinning her onto her back. He took hold of her other arm, looming over her, a knee on either side of her body to pin her down. She screamed, thrashing her limbs in a futile attempt to get away.

He laughed, and then he turned around and looked back the way they'd come, shadows blurring his features though I caught a flash of white teeth when he smiled.

'Think you can stop this happening, Belinda?'

He lashed her wrists together before pulling her to her feet, then dragged her to where a tall man shrouded in shadows waited.

The vision released me and I sat up, chest heaving, a scream building in my throat. Scott had his arms wrapped around me again and I burrowed in to him, needing to chase away the chill that enveloped me, shudders racking my body.

'It's okay, Belinda. You're okay. I've got you.'

His chest rumbled with the words, and I concentrated on the solid strength radiating from him as I calmed down.

After a long moment, I gave a sigh and eased myself out of his arms.

'What did you see?' Scott asked, barely leashed tension in his voice.

I shook my head, not sure what to tell him. It had felt like a vision, but how could that be? How could the woman's attacker know I was able to "see" what he was doing?

After a deep breath to steady my nerves, I told him what I had seen.

'So you don't think it was a vision?'

'I don't know? It felt real, but it can't be. He taunted me, asked if I thought I could stop it from happening.'

'Was there anything in it to identify where and when the attack would take place? Who the men were?'

'I couldn't see their faces, but I'm sure they're the same ones I've been seeing in my nightmares. Only in them I'm the one being chased. As for where and when, it's night and the moon is full. There are lots of trees around, but nothing familiar.'

'You've been having nightmares about these guys?' Scott's grip on my hand tightened. 'Tell me about them.'

In a low voice, not wanting Mum or Dad to overhear, I told him about being chased by one dark figure while another watched on.

'I don't like this. I don't like it at all,' he said when I'd finished.

'You and me both,' I said.

There was silence for a moment, and then Scott stood up.

'There's some people I would like you to meet, three young women I met on the job a few months back. I'm hoping one of them might be able to help us figure out if what you saw was a real vision or not.'

'How would they do that? Who are they?'

'Two of them are sisters, twins actually, and the third is a friend of theirs. They were all involved in some strange stuff, stuff there was no logical explanation for.'

'Stuff like my visions?'

'Honestly, I don't know what they can do or even if they can do anything. All I know is that some crazy doctor was convinced they had psychic abilities and was out to get them. She was declared insane after she was arrested, and locked away in a mental institution. She was crazy, no doubt about it, but from what I saw I think she was telling the truth about what her daughter and the others could do.'

Could it be true? Were there other people like me?

If they did have psychic abilities, maybe one of them would be able to tell me how to get rid of my visions?

164

'When do you want to go see them?'

'Now, if that's okay? We need to find out if your vision is going to come true. If the woman you saw is going to be kidnapped, we need to save her.'

Filled with hope and determination, I got to my feet and shuffled over to the wall, calling out to Mum as I made my way to the kitchen. 'I'm going out with Scott. I'll be back soon.'

'But that reporter is still out there,' said Mum.

'Scott can drive into the garage,' I said. It was a double garage, so there was plenty of room for his car to fit beside Dad's.

Minutes later, sunglasses on to hide my face, I was seated in the front seat of Scott's car with Dad at the open door urging me to be careful.

After he closed the door I buckled up, and then stiffened.

'This isn't a police car, is it? I don't want people to see me and think I've been arrested.'

Scott gave a low chuckle. 'No, you're good. This is my own vehicle. I'm off duty at the moment.'

A warm flush swept through me at the thought that he'd come to see me on his own time. Then there was the kiss. He'd said it was a bad idea, but it hadn't felt bad. No, it had felt amazing, up until the vision, nightmare, whatever it was hit.

'Are you ready?' Scott asked.

I gave a nod, remaining silent as he backed out of the garage. Through the closed window, I could hear the reporter shouting my name. I kept my head down and averted from the window, hating he could see me, while I had no idea who he was or how many of them were there.

'You can relax,' Scott said moments later. 'We're in the clear.'

I straightened up, tension leaving my body as the sun shining in through the windows warmed me up. Then I thought about the reason he was taking me to visit complete strangers.

While it was important we made sure the woman I saw being attacked was okay, my real focus had to be on getting rid of the visions.

It was the only way to get the reporter to leave me alone and to give me a chance of getting my life back to something that resembled normal.

Of course, if the visions were gone, there would be no more reason for Scott to have anything to do with me. I would no longer need his comforting strength. No more chance to get caught up in heady kisses.

He hadn't said anything about the kiss. Maybe it didn't mean anything to him. For all I knew, it could have been a sympathy kiss, to make me feel better about my situation. He obviously cared deeply about helping others, willing to put his life on the line to save the people from the bus accident and the apartment fire. I could just be a charity case to him.

Bottom lip caught between my teeth, I forced that thought out of my mind.

I had to focus on finding out what my vision meant and how to stop it from happening. Then there would be time to find out if Scott's interest in me was based on real affection or the circumstances pushing us together.

8

'We're here,' said Scott, speaking for the first time since we'd left my parents' house.

I kept my sunglasses on as I got out of the car, not sure what to do with my hands as I waited for him to come around and lead me to the front door. His strong hand grasped mine, our fingers entwining as he gave a low commentary on where we were and what was ahead of me so I wouldn't stumble.

I still wasn't used to being led around, but he made it feel less awkward, more like a friendly gesture rather than a chore. He gently steered me along a concrete path, an arm around my back, and positioned me in front of the door.

He knocked three times and then let go of my waist to hold my hand. I was grateful for his constant support. I was out of my element, about to meet people with strange abilities like mine. It was good to know that no matter what happened I had Scott there to back me up.

A long moment later the door opened.

'Miss Sherman, I'm not sure if you remember me. I'm Constable Scott Carlton. I was wondering if we could have a moment of your time.'

His words were met by silence, and his hand tightened around mine.

Finally, he said, 'I'm sorry, I don't understand sign language. Is your sister or Celeste home?'

'Hello, Belinda. I'm glad you came.'

I gave a start, recognising the voice as the young woman who had spoken to me at the Community Centre. 'Angel?'

'How do you know who she is?' Scott asked.

'Please ask the constable to come inside, and I'll try to explain everything,' said Angel.

Confusion washed over me. 'Why can't you ask him?'

'Because he can't hear me.'

'Belinda, what are you talking about?' Scott swung me around to face him.

I frowned, not sure what to do next. 'I don't understand why you can't hear her, but Angel has asked us to come inside.'

To Scott's credit, he didn't argue, accepting my words and leading me into the house. He led me slowly, pointing out obstacles until we reached what had to be the lounge room. He directed me to sit on a plush couch and sat beside me, still holding my hand.

'Belinda, I can talk to you using telepathy,' said Angel, 'but as I can't communicate with the constable in the same way, I'll get a whiteboard and marker so I can write down what I'm saying to save you having to repeat everything.'

I heard her leaving the room and told Scott what she was doing.

'You can really hear her, in your head?' he asked.

I nodded, thinking how crazy it was. But then so were my visions. I hoped Angel would have answers.

'That explains a lot, actually,' Scott said, and I was sure he was smiling. At least it sounded as though he was. I wished I could see him, to judge his expressions rather than having to rely on voice alone.

Angel returned and I tried to track her movements by sound. When I was sure she had sat down I asked, 'Can you read my mind?'

She gave a light laugh. 'No, telepathy doesn't work like that. I can hear your thoughts as you project them to me, and it works the same for you. I can't hear what you are thinking. Also, you don't actually need to speak out loud for me to hear you.'

'Really?'

With her encouragement I had a go at thinking my next question for her rather than saying it. 'How is any of this possible? Why can I hear you but Scott can't?'

'Only those who have had their psychic ability awakened are able to communicate via telepathy,' she said.

'Hey, are you two carrying on a conversation without me?' Scott asked.

I gave his hand a squeeze. 'Sorry. I was just testing something out. I can talk to Angel without using my voice. But I will make sure to talk so you can hear my side of the conversation at least.'

Saying it out loud didn't feel as weird as it should. Then again, I had been having visions. Time to get the conversation on track.

'At the Community Centre you said you would see me today. You knew I was going to come here, didn't you?'

'I didn't know where or why, but as soon as I saw you I knew you would be able to hear me and I'd see you today. Then, last night, when I saw the report on you, I realised you would come to see me about your visions.'

Anticipation made my voice shake. 'Does that mean you know how to stop them?'

'Hang on, I thought we came here to learn more about your visions. Not to stop you from having them.' Scott let go of my hand. 'I thought you wanted to help the woman you saw being kidnapped?'

'I do, but I can't go on like this. I want the visions to stop. I want my eyesight back. I want to be normal.'

'You are normal,' said Angel. 'Your visions are a gift,

that's all.'

'They're more of a burden than a gift. Gifts aren't meant to terrify you. I don't understand why I'm even getting them.'

A strange feeling swept over me, almost like an emotional wave of reassurance, support and sympathy. It was coming from Angel, and I filed away the knowledge that we could broadcast feelings as well as words telepathically as she started speaking.

'I've been like this since birth. Which caused a whole set of problems for me.'

Irony filled the words in my head.

'But that is another story. For you, and others like you, abilities manifest after some kind of traumatic event, like the car accident you were in. At least, that's what I think happens. Others, like me, are born with the ability to do things with their minds.'

A shudder swept through me at the memory of the accident that had claimed my sight. It didn't seem fair that it had also saddled me with an ability I didn't want. Maybe it would be different if I'd been born with an ability, like Angel, but right now it felt more like a punishment than a gift.

'Do you have visions too?' Scott asked.

'I can sometimes see events before they happen, but not as clearly as Belinda seems to be able to. I guess you could say I can do a little bit of everything, but fire is my strongest power.'

'You started the fire at the old orphanage, when that crazy doctor had you and the others locked up in that makeshift laboratory,' said Scott. 'What the hell was going on in that place?'

I sat in silence as Angel told her story, the only sound the whisk of the marker against the whiteboard as she wrote it down for Scott's benefit. He didn't say a word until she got to the part where he had shown up and arrested Dr Wood and the orderly that had tried to shoot Angel.

'Wow, that is incredible. I knew something strange was going on, but I never imagined it was on that scale,' Scott said. 'What you went through, what that crazy doctor put you through. It's amazing you've turned out so normal.'

'Of course, because telepathy and being able to throw fireballs are normal everyday activities,' I said, shaking my head.

I thought I'd been hit hard, losing my eyesight and having to endure terrifying visions. But what happened to Angel, and her friend Celeste, made my experiences pale in comparison. 'How could a mother do that to her own child?'

'Dr Wood was obsessed with proving her theory about those with psychic abilities correct, and she used her daughter as a blank subject. But we think it was her using Electro Shock Treatment on Celeste that gave her the ability to create lightning. That ability helped her to stop her mother, even if it made her a target for Dr Frankel.'

'This Dr Frankel, did they catch him?' I did not like the idea of a scientist looking to capture those with psychic abilities to turn them into weapons. My face had been plastered all over the news. What if he came after me?

'No, he managed to get away, as did the other scientists working for him. The police have no idea where he is or what he's up to. But I'm sure we haven't heard the last of him. The impression I got was that he is just as obsessed as Dr Wood with psychic abilities, although for a different reason.'

'Hang on, you said Celeste was shot. But she wasn't injured when I got there with Davidson,' said Scott.

Angel was silent for a moment and I could hear the marker moving over the whiteboard. Then she said, 'Ethan can connect with nature. It's what allows him to create

171

earthquakes, but he can also use his abilities to heal people. He saved Celeste's life.'

Body rigid, I blurted out, 'Do you think he'd be able to restore my eyesight?'

'I didn't say anything earlier, because I didn't want to get your hopes up, but it is possible. We won't know until we try. I sent him a message after you arrived.' She gave a mental shrug. 'If I'd known exactly when I would meet you I would have arranged for Andie and Celeste to be here too, but they're on a camping trip with Nick and Daniel.'

'What about Belinda's visions?' Scott asked. 'If she gets her eyesight back, won't they stop?'

'I don't believe so. From what I have observed, once someone's abilities are triggered they are there for good,' said Angel.

I scrunched up my face. There went that hope. But the visions would be easier to deal with if they weren't the only things I got to see.

Scott continued to ask Angel questions relating to when she had been held prisoner by the crazy doctor, but I found it hard to concentrate. Once this Ethan arrived, I might get my sight back. I wanted to get up and pace until he arrived. But that would mean bumping into furniture and making a fool of myself without someone to guide me, which would defeat the point of pacing off my rising excitement.

I tugged my thoughts back to the here and now when Scott asked Angel if she knew how to tell if what she "saw" was a true vision or not.

'It's hard to explain what I see. For me it's usually more of a feeling than a true vision,' she said.

I leaned forward on the couch. 'For me it's like being right there, watching it all unfold and being unable to do anything about it. Except for the last one. That was different.'

I described the vision to Angel, shuddering when I related how the attacker had turned around and taunted me.

'That is strange. Are you sure it was a vision?'

'That's why I brought Belinda here,' said Scott, after she had written her question on the whiteboard. 'She needs to know why she is having these visions and whether everything she sees is going to come true.'

'Here, let me see what you saw.'

I heard Angel get up and move toward me. I stood, reaching out for her, instinctively knowing what she meant.

We stood facing each other, clasping our hands tighter, and I thought back to the vision that had brought me here. I let it play in my head, this time not so caught up in the horror with the sense of Angel at my side, so I was able to take in more detail. After the kidnapper straddled his victim's prone body, he once again turned to face me to deliver his taunt. Even though he was looking directly at me, his features were vague and I would never be able to give an accurate description to enable him to be caught.

But my fingers itched to sketch him, to give the police something to go on.

The vision released us but Angel did not let go of my hands. She clutched them tight, and pulled me closer to her.

'This is wrong. This is not a true vision, and yet it feels like something that could come to pass. I think he sent the vision to you. He is trying to draw you out. It's you he wants, not that poor woman he was chasing.'

I let go of her hands, sinking back to the couch as Scott asked what had happened.

'He's after me,' I said. 'Angel said the vision is meant to lure me somewhere so he can capture me.'

'I won't let him touch you.' Scott wrapped his arm around me, drawing me close.

'It's more than that,' said Angel. 'I could sense someone else, someone directing him, but I couldn't get a clear picture of who it was.'

I nodded, remembering the sense I had in my nightmares that there was someone directing the man chasing me through the moonlit night. I shivered, remembering our earlier conversation, and my fear of being turned into a weapon.

'Do you think it's Dr Frankel?'

I heard Scott suck in a breath, even as a wave of horror washed toward me from Angel.

'You're right. It makes sense. And that would explain the sense of familiarity I got when I experienced your vision.'

'No, not vision. Taunt.'

'Does that mean the woman Belinda saw getting attacked is okay? That this won't happen?' Scott asked.

'I don't know,' said Angel. 'It all felt so wrong, I honestly can not tell you if it will happen or not. There was nothing to indicate where or when it might take place, or who she is. Even if it was a true vision, there was nothing in it to help us stop it from happening.'

Before I could ask anything more, a knock at the door came. I heard Angel go to answer it, and sat nervously perched on the edge of the couch.

Was this Ethan?

Would he be able to cure my blindness?

9

It was hard to sit still and not jump about when they came into the room.

'Hi, Belinda, I'm Ethan.'

I heard his greeting both with my ears and my head, and got the sense he was nervous. His next words confirmed it.

'I wish I could tell you I'm an expert at this, but so far I have only healed two people. I'm not exactly sure how it all works, but if you're willing to let me try I will see what I can do.'

I gave a quick nod, not trusting my voice.

I stilled as his hands touched my temples. Eyes closed, I waited for something, a sign he was healing me. But other than feeling warm where he was touching me, I felt nothing.

'Here, let me see.'

I felt Angel place her hands on top of Ethan's, and this time I felt a tingle beneath their combined touch. My breathing sped up. It had to be working.

They let go and I opened my eyes.

Darkness still blanketed my sight, and tears trickled down my cheeks.

'I'm sorry,' said Ethan. 'I wish I could help you, but it appears this isn't the kind of injury I can heal.'

I nodded, wiping my face and turning away.

Warm arms wrapped around me and I sank into Scott's embrace. Several deep breaths later I was able to speak. 'It's okay. I guess I'm not meant to get my sight back.'

A mobile phone rang, and Scott let go of me.

'Constable Carlton,' he said.

A moment later he handed the phone to me.

'Belinda, honey, you need to come home right away.' Mum's voice bubbled with excitement.

'Why, what's going on?'

'We just got a call from Dr Phillips. He has been in touch with an eye specialist and he thinks you would be a good candidate for an experimental surgery that could restore your eyesight.'

I started crying again, not sure whether to believe in the good fortune after being disappointed once already. If Ethan, with his abilities, couldn't heal me then how was a doctor supposed to do it?

'Belinda, are you still there?'

I sucked in a breath. 'Yes, I'm here. I'll be home soon.'

'Oh, honey, wouldn't it be wonderful if they can fix your eyes?'

Yes. Yes it would.

If it actually happened.

If this wasn't just another instance of false hope.

I handed the phone back to Scott, and told him and the others what Mum had said.

We said goodbye to Angel and Ethan, promising to return as soon as we could. Angel, in particular, was concerned about what my last vision meant and if it was connected to Dr Frankel and his weapons program. I didn't blame her for being concerned. Knowing he was out there, hunting those who had psychic abilities, was freaking me out.

I resolved to put the possibility out of my mind, to forget all about my vision for a moment. It was time to focus on me, and finding out if I was a candidate for the experimental surgery Dr Phillip had called Mum about.

That was easier said than done when a new vision hit

soon after Scott started the car.

I stiffened, hands forming claws on my lap as it played out in front of me.

A small child, running across the road after a red ball, a car coming around the corner with the sun's glare blocking the driver's view. Too late, the driver saw the child and applied the brakes. The car screeched to a halt, but not before clipping the child and sending the small body flying in the air to land on the road in a crumpled heap as the ball rolled slowly down the gutter.

I came back to myself and reached out to grab Scott's arm as the details spilled from my mouth.

'It happened on the corner of Hampton and Conroy Streets. You have to hurry. We don't have much time.'

Now I wished we were seated in a police car, regardless of whether people thought I'd been arrested, as Scott wove through traffic as fast as he could. We had to make it. I kept seeing the small child's broken body lying in the middle of the road, the worried face of the driver who had hit him as she climbed from the car and ran toward him.

We had to stop it from happening.

'We're almost there,' said Scott, tension filling his voice as he accelerated around a corner. Then he stopped the car and jumped out.

I was left there, waiting in the dark, not sure what was happening. Had we been in time? Had he saved the child?

Then a second vision hit.

This one showed a tall young man racing toward a small child playing with a red ball on the footpath. It took me a moment to realise what I was looking at. This had to be Scott and the little boy I'd seen get hit by a car. As I watched on, the ball fell from the boy's hands and rolled toward the road as he ran after it. Then I saw the car from my earlier vision coming around the corner and Scott diving into the middle of the road to pluck the child to safety just before it would have run into him.

I sagged back in the seat, waiting for the vision to release me, sure it was all fine.

But the vision continued, showing Scott with the boy in his arms as he reached the safety of the footpath and handed him to a frantic mother. Scott shrugged off her thanks and headed back to the other side of the road, to where I waited in the car. Then came the sound of screeching brakes as another car appeared out of nowhere and slammed into Scott. His body was thrown up and over the bonnet, and then slid to the ground as the car came to a shuddering halt, head twisted at an impossible angle.

No.

I had to stop it from happening.

I couldn't let Scott be killed.

I got out of the car, shouting his name.

I heard a screech of brakes, for real this time, but didn't know if it was the first car or the second one. I ran a hand along the side of the car as I made my way to the bonnet, still calling out for Scott and getting no response. I could hear yelling in the distance, ahead of me, but I couldn't leave the relative safety of the car.

If I let go and walked on I could end up in the middle of the road myself. I shook my head, torn by indecision. How was I going to save Scott?

I could hear a car coming from behind me and I let go of the bonnet, sure this was the one that would run Scott down. I stepped into the middle of the road, at least I think that's where I was, waving my hands to flag it down.

More voices could be heard, coming closer, so many of them it was hard to distinguish individual voices.

A hand gripped my arm, tugging me to the left.

'It's okay, Belinda.' The voice was muffled, indistinct.

With the noise of so many people around me, and the revving of a nearby car engine, it was hard to tell who had spoken, but an image popped into my head of Scott leading me to safety. Relieved he was okay, I let him lead me back to his car.

People brushed against me as I walked, some of them knocking me sideways in their haste. Scott put his arm around my waist, pulling me closer, and I frowned when his aftershave tickled my nose. It was strong, musky, not like the fresh clean scent I usually associated with him.

'Is the little boy okay?' I asked, raising my voice to be heard above the din of people.

He didn't answer, walking faster. I stumbled over my feet in my effort to keep up with him. His grip on my waist tightened.

I heard someone call my name from behind us, panic evident. It was Scott's voice.

But if he was behind me, then who had hold of me?

I tried to pull free. 'Stop. Who are you?'

He still didn't speak, just pulled me along with him, moving even faster. I slammed into something hard. A car.

I heard the door open and whoever had hold of me tried to push me inside.

I twisted in his grip, lashing out with my hands, hearing a grunt when I connected with his chest.

But he didn't let go. He wrenched me closer, hand on my head as he tried to push me into his car.

'Let her go.'

At Scott's shout, the man holding on to me suddenly shoved me backward. I flailed my arms, tripping over something and landing on my butt. I heard the slamming of a car door a moment before an engine roared to life.

Strong arms enveloped me, holding me tight, Scott's familiar fresh scent washing over me.

'Are you okay?'

I sagged into his embrace, shaking. 'I don't know.' Tears spilled down my cheeks and he held me as I cried.

Then I stiffened, pulling away. 'Is he all right? The little boy?'

'It's fine. He's fine. I got him out of the way of the car.' Scott's voice shook. 'Then I turned around and saw some guy leading you away. God, Belinda. I thought I'd lost you.'

'I'll be okay. But what about you? I saw a car hit you.'

Even as I said it, I gave a start. The vision of Scott being hit had felt different. I hadn't realised it at the time, but it had been more like the nightmare where I had been taunted by the man attacking the woman in the woods. I sucked in a breath. Was that who had tried to get me into his car?

'Is that why you got out of the car? You had a vision?'

'I'm not sure what it was now. But yes, I was trying to save you.'

His arms tightened around me.

'I can look after myself. It was dangerous for you to get out of the car. There was a lot of traffic around. It could have been you who got hit. I should never have left you alone.'

'If you had, it would have been the little boy who got hit.'

He sighed, the movement rumbling through his body. 'You're right, but this still shouldn't have happened. If I'd been a moment later that guy would have had you in his car and driven off.' Tension laced his words. 'Did he say anything? I need to go to the station to file a report, get them looking for him.'

I shook my head. 'After he first spoke, he didn't say anything else. Did you get a good look at him?'

'I only saw him from the back. He was tall, about my height. Close cropped, dark blonde hair, wearing dark jeans and a black long sleeve shirt.'

I could hear the frustration in his words.

'Not much to go on.'

'I think it was the guy from my vision. The one who taunted me.' It was the only thing that made sense. Who else would be after me?

'I need to get you home. Keep you safe. If he's tried to abduct you once, he'll probably try again.'

I shivered. Abduct. Having him say it made it hit home. Someone had tried to kidnap me. A man who had taunted me in a vision.

I said little as Scott directed me back to his car and drove me home. After he left me in Mum and Dad's hands, urging them to keep the doors locked and to be vigilant, he headed to the police station to tell his superiors what had happened. He wanted them to assign me a guard, in case the guy tried to kidnap me again. But even as he'd filled me in on his plan, I could hear in his voice that he didn't think he would be successful. Not with so little to go on.

But I had no time to sit and think it through. Minutes after Scott left the phone rang and it was Dr Phillips, saying we had to be up at the hospital in half an hour to meet with the eye specialist.

I wished Scott could be there too, if only for his support and solid presence. I had Mum and Dad sitting on either side of me in the waiting room at the Vision Centre, but still felt vulnerable after what had happened at the accident scene.

Dr Phillips was on hand to greet us when we arrived, and he quickly introduced us to the specialist, Dr Randle, before the two of them disappeared into an examination room to get everything ready for the test. After a tense wait, Mum, Dad and I were ushered in and I followed Dr Randle's instructions, opening my eyes wide as she presumably shone a torch into them to allow her to see the damage that had been done. After several photos were taken of the back of my eyes, we returned to the waiting room to await the final verdict.

Finally, Dr Phillips led us to Dr Randle's office to find out once and for all if there was any chance of restoring my sight.

10

'Belinda,' said Dr Randle, 'from what I can see you would be a perfect candidate for the surgery. If you are willing to give it a go, I can book you in for tomorrow morning.'

So soon.

It was crazy. This was what I wanted, but I hadn't expected it to take place so quickly. Excitement thrummed through my body at the thought I might have my eyesight back in less than twenty-four hours.

'The procedure will take at least two hours, and you must realise there are no guarantees. What I am proposing to do could have no effect on your eyesight at all, or it might lead to only partial improvement.'

'Even partial improvement would have to be better than not being able to see at all,' I said.

'So you want to go ahead with the procedure? You understand the risks involved?'

Dr Randle had run through the risks associated with any kind of eye surgery. Seeing as I was already blind, I didn't think any of them sounded that bad. Not that I wanted to get an eye infection, or lose my eyes completely, but the chances of that happening were minimal.

'I want to do it.'

'Excellent. I will go and get the paperwork sorted while Dr Phillips runs through the pre-op information and after care that will be required.'

She left the room and I struggled to concentrate on Dr Phillips's words as he explained the regime I would have to follow after the surgery. Daily eye drops for up to six months and no strenuous exercise for two weeks did not sound like a tough challenge, not if the end result was that I could see again.

Head in a whirl, I left the office and let Mum and Dad's excited chatter wash over me as we made our way back to the car. I had no idea how I would be able to sleep that night, anticipation for the coming operation sure to keep me awake.

Angel didn't think getting my eyesight back would stop the visions, much as I wished it would. Scott would be disappointed if I could no longer use my visions to help people, but that was a price I was more than willing to pay to be normal again.

But for now I pushed all of that out of my mind. Tonight I was going to celebrate with my family.

I was going to get my eyesight back.

Despite Dr Randle's words urging me to understand that there were no guarantees, I was sure the surgery would work.

It had to.

Scott was right about one thing. Being blind made me vulnerable.

If someone was after me, I needed to be able to see them coming to have any hope of protecting myself.

My head was still in a whirl when we returned home. But the daze quickly fled when we found Scott waiting for us.

'Where have you been?' he asked, his hand clasping mine. 'I was worried something had happened to you.'

'Something did happen. Something wonderful,' said Mum before I could answer. 'Belinda is going to have surgery that could restore her eyesight.'

'That's great news,' he said. 'The sooner you are able to see the better.'

'What's wrong?' I asked.

'They refused my request for protection for you. Detective Johnson didn't believe you were in any danger. He thinks it is all a ploy for publicity.'

'I don't want the publicity I already have. Why would I want more?'

'Nothing short of you being attacked right in front of him would convince him otherwise. Even then he'd probably accuse you of setting it up.'

I let him lead me over to the couch. 'What are we going to do then? I can't stay cooped up inside the house, waiting for that guy to have another attempt at kidnapping me.'

'Don't worry, I won't let anything happen to you.'

While his assertion warmed my heart, I knew he couldn't protect me all the time.

Then he said, 'I've taken a leave of absence from work. Until we catch this guy, I'm going to be keeping an eye on you. I'll stake out the house, if I have to, to make sure you're okay.'

More warmth washed over me at the thought of having him as my bodyguard, the image that conjured up in my mind thanks to Grace's comment making me flush. I ducked my head, hoping he couldn't see my reaction to his words.

I focused on the logistics of the situation. 'If you are sitting in your car, watching the house, that reporter will know something is up, which could get you in trouble with your superiors. We need a better solution than that. You can stay here.'

Before I could second guess myself I called out to Mum. 'Can you make up the spare room for Scott? He's going to be keeping an eye on us for a while.'

'That's a wonderful idea. I'll put out a fresh towel for you.'

The relief in Mum's voice echoed mine.

I felt so much better knowing Scott was going to be just down the hall from me, never more than a few steps away at any time. Of course, the thought of how close he would be again sent a flush through my body. Damn Grace, for her suggestions. Good thing she wasn't here, or she'd be flirting with him for sure.

On cue there came a knock on the door, and moments later Grace was perched on the couch beside me, animatedly filling Scott in on her day at the vet surgery. He seemed happy to listen, but no more so than was appropriate and from Grace's voice she seemed content to just talk, with none of the flirting she'd employed last time.

When Scott excused himself to go home to collect his gear, I turned to Grace. 'What happened? I thought you liked him?'

'I do. He's a nice guy, and seriously good looking, but there was no point in me even trying to get his interest when he is so clearly hooked on you.'

'What are you talking about?' Even as I said it, I could feel the flush creeping over my face.

'Don't give me that. You know exactly what I'm talking about. The guy could hardly take his eyes off you. I could have been a statue for all the attention he paid me.'

'He's just looking out for me, that's all.'

'Are you kidding me? No way is that why he's here. Guys do not take leave so they can become bodyguards for girls they don't care about.'

'He's a police officer. It's his job to take care of people.'

'There's taking care of people, and then there's taking care of a girl he's interested in. Trust me, this is definitely a case of the latter.'

Mum came in then to tell us dinner was ready, saving me from replying, but even as we discussed the upcoming

186

operation over our meal, I couldn't stop thinking about Grace's words. Was I kidding myself?

Scott had kissed me, sure, but he hadn't done anything since to show that he was interested in me. Could I afford to get caught up in thinking he cared more about me than as a police officer doing his best to protect someone in danger?

I thought back on all our interactions. He had gone out of his way to be there for me, taking me to see Angel and going against his superiors to be my bodyguard. Was Grace right, and he had more in mind than just doing the right thing?

With no more to go on than one kiss, it was hard for me to be sure of his intentions. Besides, who would want to get involved with a blind girl who had visions? It had to be his career that influenced his decisions and his desire to help people. I just wished I could see him, read his expressions, so I could judge for myself what he thought about me.

As for me, what did I feel?

I felt safe when he was around, protected. And I'd certainly been blown away by his kiss. But I needed more than that to even contemplate feelings for him. I had to go by what he said and did.

Scott returned when Grace and I were doing the dishes. Mum quickly sat him down to eat the dinner she had set aside for him, ignoring his assertion that he had already eaten. Grace said a quick goodbye and then left, saying she had an early start in the morning. Mum and Dad retreated to the lounge to watch their favourite crime show, leaving me in the dining room with Scott, sipping a cup of hot chocolate.

I felt drained, having trouble keeping my eyes open, and yet strangely wired to have him there, in my parents' house, knowing he was going to be sleeping in the room next to mine. Especially after my conversation with Grace.

I was twisting my brain inside out as I analysed

everything Scott said for a hidden meaning. But soon I got caught up in the conversation as he filled me in on what it had been like growing up in a house with three much younger brothers.

'Wow, it sounds like they kept you and your mum on your toes. I can't believe three little boys could get into so much trouble.'

'You have no idea. I'm only telling you half the stuff they got into. Not even Mum knows everything. If she knew the full truth, she would have tied them to their beds and never let them leave the house. Which would have driven me crazy. It was hard enough studying as it was, without the three of them underfoot all the time.'

I gave a laugh, picturing Scott as a teenager, watching over his brothers. 'Is that what prompted you to become a police officer, all your experience keeping your brothers out of trouble?'

There was silence for a moment. Then he said, 'My father was a police officer. He was killed in the line of duty when I was twelve.'

'Oh, Scott, I'm so sorry.' I reached across the table, searching for his hand, before I could think it through. I had no idea where his hand was.

Then he took hold of my hand, squeezing it lightly.

'Thanks. It was hard, losing him. I was angry for so long, drove Mum crazy with it, but it was seeing her try to cope raising the four of us that snapped me out of it. Acting like a brat was making it harder for her, and my brothers were just as bad. They were confused, not angry, but they got into all sorts of trouble.'

'So you stepped in, helped your mum look after them.'

'Somebody had to. She had enough to deal with, keeping a roof over our heads and food on the table. Not to mention keeping us clothed. We were all growing so fast, she had to keep buying new clothes to keep up with us.'

We sat there, holding hands, for a long moment. Then I heard Mum coming into the dining area and I pulled my hand away. 'I often wondered what it would have been like to have a brother or sister. But then, I had Grace. We've spent so much time together it almost feels like we are siblings rather than just cousins or friends.'

After that, it was time to get ready for bed, and I was grateful I hadn't had any visions since the one that afternoon. Part of me still hoped Angel was wrong and that the operation to restore my sight would stop the visions. But then I felt bad for thinking that way. Scott had sacrificed so much; first to help his mum raise his brothers, and then going into a career as a police officer to help complete strangers. And here he was, staying in the room next door so he could protect me, against his superiors' wishes.

I would have to take it one day at a time. First to see if the operation was successful, and then to worry about my visions.

That was easier said than done. No sooner had I dropped off to sleep than a nightmare, vision, something, hit.

I was again running through the woods, the long white gown tangling in the bushes and slowing me down. I could see, but my vision was blurred, as if it was more of an afterimage than an actual image. The moon shone in the night sky and I used it to guide my flight as I fought to get away from whoever was chasing me. But like the woman in the vision I'd had the day before, I tripped over a tree root and fell to the ground.

A heavy body slammed into the ground beside me, and my arm was grasped. I was twisted over onto my back and a dark figure straddled my body and pinned me to the ground. I got the impression of dark eyes and close cropped blonde hair as he loomed over me.

'I'm coming for you, Belinda. Don't think your cop boyfriend can save you.'

'Why are you doing this?' I thrashed my body, trying to dislodge him.

'I have no choice. It's you or me. And I pick you.' He raised his fist and slammed it into my temple.

11

Pain flooded my head, waking me. I sat up, darkness once more enveloping me as the false sight I possessed in my nightmare vanished.

I was in my room, but I was not alone.

Someone loomed over me. I could hear breathing, and I lashed out, punching the intruder in the stomach as I got ready to scramble off the bed and bolt for the door.

'Ouch, that hurt,' said Scott.

I froze. 'Oh my God. Are you okay?' I reached out to touch him, my hand connecting with his bare chest.

Soft skin covered hard muscle, and while I was sure my cheeks had to be flaming I couldn't bring myself to pull my hand away. Instead, I ran it over the planes of his stomach, rubbing away the hurt I'd caused.

He let out a soft groan and I snatched my hand back. 'I'm so sorry. I didn't mean to hurt you. I didn't realise it was you.'

He groaned again and sank onto the bed beside me. I heard a rustling sound, as though he was running a hand through his hair.

'It's fine. I should have said something. I heard you call out, and was just coming to check you were okay. Didn't mean to scare you.'

'Guess we both scared each other,' I said, my arm brushing against his when I reached up to comb through the tangles in my hair, conscious of his body so close to mine, warm and inviting.

I swallowed and pulled my mind back from wondering

what he looked like. In a low voice, not wanting to wake Mum and Dad and have them come in and find us together, I told him what I had seen.

'You think it was like before, a vision of what could come to pass, the way Angel said?'

'I don't think so. This felt personal, like a message.' I closed my eyes and thought back to what I had seen, trying to analyse it without the fear that had overwhelmed me while I'd been experiencing it for the first time.

The man's voice, the way he'd said it had to be me or him. There had been something there, a hint of desperation. I'd again had the sense of someone else present, hidden in the shadows.

'I think he's scared. I don't think he wants to hurt me, not really, but he thinks he has no choice.' I told Scott how I thought someone else was directing his actions.

'There's always a choice. Choosing to hurt someone else to protect yourself is the wrong one.'

For the first time, I felt sympathy for my attacker. 'What if he really doesn't have a choice? I got the sense he was in a lot of pain. Pain can make people do crazy things, to make it stop.'

'Still, to hurt someone else is never right.'

I smiled. Of course he would think that way. He was the ultimate big brother, looking after his younger siblings and keeping them out of trouble, protecting the citizens of Easton, and going out of his way to protect me.

Then I frowned. 'He knows you're here with me.'

'What? How do you know that?'

I stalled before saying, 'He said my cop boyfriend wouldn't be able to protect me.'

I inwardly cringed to be labelling him as my boyfriend, even though I was only repeating what the shadow man had said.

Scott's arm wrapped around me.

'He's wrong. I won't let anything happen to you.'

While I appreciated the sentiment, and that he didn't say anything about being called my boyfriend, I had a feeling he would not be able to stop what was coming. The nightmare had a sense of inevitability to it, making me think that sooner or later I would come face to face with the man who had tried to kidnap me. In the meantime, I snuggled into Scott's arms, eager for the sense of security he gave me now, even if it wouldn't last.

After a long moment, where I listened to his even breathing, I pulled away. 'I'd better try and get back to sleep. I have a big day tomorrow.'

Scott left, and I curled up under the covers. Tomorrow I was going to find out if my sight was going to be restored. If the operation failed, I would have to spend the rest of my life in the dark, easy prey for those who were after me.

Despite the thoughts roaming through my head, I did manage to fall asleep, waking to the sound of Mum entering my room early in the morning.

'Belinda, honey, it's time to get up. You don't want to be late.'

No, I did not.

I jumped out of bed and let Mum help me choose my clothes. After a quick trip to the bathroom, I made my way to the kitchen and accepted the steaming hot cup of tea and two slices of Vegemite toast Mum set out for me at the breakfast bar.

It wasn't until I heard Scott thank her for her hospitality, that I realised he was here as well.

His shoulder nudged mine.

'You ready for this?'

'I hope so,' I said.

A short time later breakfast was done, I'd brushed my teeth, and we were out the door. Scott had chosen to follow us in his own car, to make sure we weren't being followed.

The reporter, with no new visions making the news, had finally given up on getting the scoop and left, meaning we didn't have any spectators as Dad backed the car out of the garage. Mum and Dad chatted all the way to the Vision Centre, but I remained silent. I was too keyed up by what was about to happen to want to talk.

When we arrived, a nurse came and led me into a special waiting room while the receptionist got Mum and Dad settled in a visitors' area with the promise of tea and coffee. Scott wasn't there yet. He must have got caught in traffic.

The nurse led me over to a chair and after I was seated she pressed a small paper cup into my hand.

'This is a mild sedative, to help keep you relaxed while Dr Randle performs the surgery.'

She handed me a bottle of water and I swallowed the little pill.

'That will take effect in about half an hour and I'll come collect you when Dr Randle is ready. Once we get you settled in the operating room, she'll place anaesthetic drops into your eyes and then apply clamps to keep them open during the procedure. It won't hurt, but you may feel some pressure. That's perfectly normal, and nothing to worry about.'

I nodded, vaguely remembering Dr Randle and Dr Phillips going through all of this the day before. Still, the nurse continued.

'Once the procedure has been completed, your eyes will be covered with bandages that need to remain in place for twenty-four hours to protect them while they begin the healing process. Then you will return here tomorrow morning and we'll remove them and Dr Randle will assess your condition.'

I fought to keep my face blank, not looking forward to having to wait another day to find out if the procedure worked. But I understood the need to have my eyes covered to protect them from infection, even if the delay would chafe.

'I'll see you soon, Belinda.'

The nurse patted my shoulder and left the room, leaving me alone. I wondered if Scott had arrived yet. He would have to sit in the visitors' area with Mum and Dad, almost as if he really was my boyfriend. No one but the medical team and the patient were allowed in the operating room.

My head drooped, drowsiness sweeping over me and I struggled to keep my eyes open. So much for a mild sedative. It reminded me of the tablets my mother had given me instead of headache ones. I struggled to stay awake, to not fall asleep as I waited for the nurse to come back. It was hard without something to occupy my mind.

I could hear a television playing somewhere nearby, probably the visitors' area where Mum, Dad and Scott were. They probably had magazines to read too, while I had nothing. Not that television or magazines would do me any good without working eyes.

After what seemed like hours, I heard someone enter the room and cross to my side. A cool hand touched my arm.

'They're ready for you now, Belinda.'

I struggled to my feet, appreciating the steadying hand of the nurse as she waited until I was ready to walk. She led me along, letting me know where we were going and what we were passing as we went. She'd obviously done this a lot of times before, and I relaxed at the knowledge I was in good hands.

A whoosh sounded as an electric sliding door opened and

a waft of cool, sterile air hit me. The nurse gave my arm a gentle tug and led me over to the bed where I would lie for the procedure, helping me to clamber up onto the hard rubber mattress.

I shivered when it touched the bare parts of my skin, focusing on the sounds of people moving around me. A chair scraped and the nurse placed her hand back on my arm. 'Dr Randle will be in soon and we'll get started. I'll be sitting beside you the whole time,' she said, patting my arm. 'There's no need to be afraid.'

I wasn't afraid. Anxious, wanting it over with already so I could know if the procedure worked, but not afraid.

I wanted to tell her so, but my tongue felt woolly, the same as my head, and I was worried I'd trip over my words. So I just gave a nod instead, hoping she was watching me and saw it. Then I closed my eyes as I heard the sliding door open once more.

The nurse stood up. 'Who are you?'

'Relax, my dear,' said a man's voice. 'I'm a colleague of Dr Randle's. She has asked me to assist her with the procedure. This is my assistant, to help keep an eye on things.'

The nurse moved away, and I could hear her conversing with the newcomers in low tones. I tried to focus on what they were saying. All I could hear was a word here and there, but from the tone of the nurse's voice she was not happy about the change in situation.

'Belinda, run. Get out of there.'

I gasped at the sound of Angel's voice in my head. What was going on? I struggled into a sitting position.

'You're in danger. You need to get out of there now.'

At Angel's words I swung my legs over the side of the bed.

I heard a loud cry followed by a bang, and then rough hands grabbed hold of my shoulders and pushed me back down to the bed.

I fought to break free, calling out for help, but a hand covered my mouth and smothered my cries. Terror swamped through me at the sound of a harsh laugh.

'You're not going anywhere, Belinda.'

I recognised the voice. The man from my nightmare. The one chasing me through the woods.

A sharp sting in my left shoulder made me wince, and then the dizziness hit me tenfold. Head swimming, I feebly tried to push him away, but my efforts were useless.

I could feel my body being arranged on the bed, my hands folded across my chest. 'She's all good to go, Dr Frankel.'

'Thank you, Lachlan.'

'Can I have it now? Please? The pain is killing me.' His voice was threaded with desperation.

'I'm afraid that will have to wait until after the procedure and we are clear of here. I don't want to risk you becoming distracted. But don't worry, my boy, I promise I will give you your pain medication as soon as we are finished here.'

Cool hands gripped my head.

'She's a pretty little thing. It's a shame we have to mar her beauty, but I cannot risk her losing her ability to see the future.'

I fought to make sense of his words, shuddering as cold metal touched the area around my left eye. He pried my eye open and then whatever he'd put around it held it that way. Then he repeated the process with the right eye. I stared sightlessly up, feeling a watery sensation as some kind of drops were placed in both eyes.

The anaesthetic drops Dr Randle had spoken about?

None of this made sense.

Where was Dr Randle? How would the procedure to restore my eyesight mar my supposed beauty?

The hand had been removed from my mouth and I tried to speak, to ask them what was going on, but all that came out was an unintelligible sigh.

A hand patted my arm.

'Just relax, my dear,' said the man Lachlan had called Dr Frankel. 'The procedure will be over before you know it, and then you'll never have to worry about your eyes again.'

It was hard to think, lethargy pulling me under. That name. Dr Frankel. I'd heard it before, recently. I couldn't remember where. I said the name over and over in my head, hoping it would jog my memory.

'Hang on, Belinda. Help is on its way.'

'Angel,' I said, the word slipping past my lips on a sigh.

'Did she just say Angel?' Lachlan asked.

'I'm afraid so. It seems we don't have as long as I'd hoped. We need to hurry. Those pesky girls could be on their way now. I'd wanted to take my time, extracting her eyes, but now I'm going to have to get messy.'

Horror swamped me as the meaning of his words sank in.

Dr Frankel was the scientist who had wanted to turn Angel and the others into weapons. And he wasn't here to fix my eyes.

He wanted to take them out.

12

I tried to move, to get away, but someone held me down as I felt pressure against my left eye.

No, I couldn't let him take them.

A loud groan sounded nearby, and at first I thought it was coming from me.

Then Dr Frankel said, 'Lachlan, the nurse is coming around. Take care of her.'

The pressure against my chest eased as Lachlan went to see to the nurse, but I still couldn't move. I let out a whimper as the pressure against my left eye increased.

'I'm sorry, Belinda, but this is the best way to preserve your abilities. Without eyes to distract you, you will be able to focus more on your duties. You and Lachlan will make a wonderful team.'

Lachlan returned, and said, 'Dr Frankel, we need to leave now. She must have somehow reached out to that Angel chick and called in reinforcements. I just had a vision of the cop boyfriend storming in here in five minutes, tops. Seems the distraction we arranged for him didn't work.'

I felt a thrill at the realisation Scott was coming to save me.

'Quick, pick her up. We'll take her with us,' said Dr Frankel.

No.

I was scooped off the bed and carried away. A door opened, not the sliding one, and a faint groan came from somewhere nearby. Then there was silence filled only with the sound of breathing as Lachlan held me close to his chest. I tried to talk, to beg him to let me go, but the words couldn't come.

But maybe I didn't need words. I had been able to talk to Angel without using my voice. If Lachlan was like me, able to see future events, maybe I could talk to him the same way.

I had no idea how to reach out to him, my thoughts still muddled from the sedative and whatever drug I'd been given to keep me immobile, but I gave it a go.

'Lachlan, can you hear me?'

There was no response to my mental voice. I had no idea if I was even sending it out. But I gave it another try.

'Please, you have to help me.'

I concentrated on trying to push my voice into his mind. I felt a numbing wash of emotions surround me, a black abyss that sucked in all light and sound.

His thoughts were a muddle, confused and hurt, locked away in the kernel of his being. A layer of guilt overlapped it all, remorse for what Dr Frankel was making him do. The one clear thought that came through was that he had to do it, to make the pain stop.

His stride lengthened and I now felt warm air on my face. We had to be outside the building. Tears pricked my eyes, still clamped open.

I had to get through to Lachlan before it was too late. 'Please, I know you don't want to hurt me. Help me, and I promise I will try to help you too.'

I felt a mental flinch coming from the mass of confusion in his head. But then I was thrust out, unable to know if he had heard me or not.

His arms tightened around me, his steps jagged as he quickened his pace.

I heard a shout from behind us, Scott calling my name. I

sucked in a breath, marshalling the last of my energy to struggle weakly in Lachlan's arms. Still drugged and finding it almost impossible to move, all I could do was unbalance him. I sent a wave of thought into his head, adding to his confusion, making him stumble.

He went down and I tumbled from his arms, barely feeling the impact as I hit the ground and rolled onto my side.

More shouting followed and then came the sound of an engine roaring off and running footsteps.

Soon I was rolled onto my back, Scott's voice murmuring my name as he scooped me into his arms and cradled me to his chest.

'Oh my God, Belinda.'

I burrowed my head into his shoulder, letting the tension slip out of my body. I was safe.

After a moment he released me slightly and his warm hands worked to dislodge the clamps keeping my eyes open. I blinked, eyes watering. Thanks to the drops and the drugs I'd been given they didn't hurt, but I'm sure being open for so long would have made them red and irritated. But none of that mattered.

I was in Scott's arms. He'd saved me.

He gently began to question me about what had happened, but I was still having trouble speaking. Soon he stopped, getting to his feet with me still cradled in his arms, and a short time later I felt the coolness of being indoors once more. I was placed back on a bed and resisted his attempts to lay me down, remembering the helplessness I'd felt when Dr Frankel had me in his clutches.

'It's okay, I won't let anything happen to you.'

'How did you know I needed you?' I was finally able to ask.

'Ethan called me. He said Angel had contacted him

telepathically and told him I needed to get here immediately, that something bad was going to happen to you during the procedure. He didn't have any details, but I got here as fast as I could. I got here just in time to see some guy carrying you out of a side door.'

He squeezed me tight.

'He said you were delayed, that they'd arranged a way to keep you away.'

'He? Who were they?'

'Lachlan, he's the one from my nightmares. The guy who wanted to cut my eyes out was Dr Frankel.'

He stiffened, the arm around me holding me so tightly it was almost painful.

'He was going to cut out your eyes?'

In a soft voice, I told him what had happened. 'I don't know what happened to Dr Randle and the nurse. Are they okay?'

'They were both drugged. Dr Randle was in the side room they took you through. The nurse was on the floor of the theatre. They were both coming round as I ran through, but they seemed to be otherwise unharmed. I left your mum and dad with them.'

He went silent. 'You're sure it was Dr Frankel?'

'Yes, it was him all right.' I shuddered at the thought of being in his clutches, forced to become a weapon as he appeared to have forced Lachlan.

Scott hugged me and I was content to let him as more people entered the room. He didn't let go until Dr Phillips arrived and checked me over to make sure I hadn't sustained any injuries in the fall. He stayed beside me the entire time.

Finally, Dr Phillips pronounced I was fine to go home. 'It will take a few hours for the sedative you've been given to wear off completely, as with the drug to keep you immobile, but there should be no lasting effect. Your young man here can bring you up to the hospital if you display any adverse reactions, but I'm sure you'll be fine.'

'Thank you, Dr Phillips. How are Dr Randle and the nurse?' I asked as Scott helped me off the bed. I leaned into him, appreciating his support with my legs still unsteady.

'They're going to be fine. The nurse is recovering from the effects of the sedative she was given, while Dr Randle has a bump on the back of her head and a slight concussion. She asked me to apologise to you for the need to delay the procedure. After everything that has happened this morning, she'll need a day to recover. But we can schedule it in for tomorrow morning.'

I gave a nod, the procedure the least of my concerns. In fact, I wasn't sure if I wanted to go through with it again. The thought of lying on the bed, helpless, not sure if the doctor carrying out the procedure was there to restore my sight or remove my eyes; it might take me longer than a day to get over that. But I still wanted my sight back, so I guess that meant I would have to put my faith in Dr Randle and hope that next time nothing bad happened.

'I'll be with Belinda, tomorrow, while she undergoes the procedure,' said Scott, his words firm and not inviting debate. 'I'm not letting her out of my sight with that crazy doctor out to get her.'

Warmth flooded my body and I sagged against him. His calm assertion washed my fears away. Yes, I would go through with the procedure and I would not let fear of what had almost happened stop me from following through on my plan.

Scott ushered me out to where Mum and Dad were in the waiting room.

It was funny, after everything that had happened, to know

it had been Scott by my side the entire time I'd been checked over by Dr Phillips and not my parents. It was as if even they realised that I needed to be with him.

They made no protest when Scott said he would drive me home, after a stop to see Angel.

But it wasn't just Angel waiting for us.

I could hear a commotion in my head when I was ushered inside her house with Scott at my side. A bubble of voices silently conversing.

Then they spoke out loud and I was introduced to Angel's twin sister, Andie, and their friend Celeste. These were the ones Dr Frankel had kidnapped.

I sank on to the couch, Scott holding one of my hands, a hot cup of coffee in the other thanks to Andie, and listened as they explained in more detail about what had happened to them just over a month ago.

Ethan was there too, and he did something to remove the last vestiges of the drugs I'd been given from my body. It felt like fire rushing through my veins, burning the drugs away. With the three girls he barely managed to get a word in, although each time he spoke I could hear his affection for Angel in his voice. For Scott's benefit, the conversation was mostly verbal with the others translating Angel's sign language for him.

'He's not going to give up, is he?' I asked during a lull in the conversation. 'He seems determined to go ahead with his weapons project and it looks as though he's singled me out as his next candidate.'

'I'm afraid so,' said Angel. 'I can't see clearly what he plans, as it involves us as well.'

That was a horrible thought, but at the same time it made me feel less alone to know I wasn't the only target.

'I knew he'd turn up again, but I don't like the sound of

this guy he has working with him,' said Celeste.

'I don't think Lachlan has much of a choice. He was in a lot of pain, and Dr Frankel promised to give him medication after he helped him kidnap me.' The memory of the confusion and hurt swirling through Lachlan's mind made me wince. 'I think Dr Frankel is using the pain medication as a way of controlling him.'

'I wouldn't put it past him,' said Andie. 'Look at the way he lied to Celeste's crazy mother about the project being run by her, to get her to do what he wanted.'

I felt the mental wince that came from Celeste at the mention of her mother. Every time she spoke, both verbally and mentally, I got the image of lightning flashing over a night sky in my head. With Ethan it was a rumble of earth and the clean scent after a rain shower.

It seemed unbelievable that these people could create lightning or an earthquake, manipulate it with their minds, but I guess that was no less strange than being able to see future events.

'What are we going to do? How are we supposed to find him when the police have had no luck for the last month?' Andie's voice came tinged with a sense of deep strength, her firm character and need to protect her sister shining through.

'We need to find this Lachlan and get him away from Dr Frankel. If he has abilities that are being abused, we have to help him.'

'You're too soft, Angel,' said Andie. 'You always want to save people. The guy was willing to stand there and let Dr Frankel cut out Belinda's eyes. I don't care what kind of hold Frankel has on him, only a monster would do that.'

'It's not that simple,' I said. 'I agree with Angel. He needs help.'

'But first we have to find him,' said Ethan.

'I'm sure that won't be a problem. If what I'm sensing is correct, he'll soon come after Belinda again,' said Angel.

'And I'll be ready for him,' said Scott. 'Angel, you said you haven't been able to see anything, but what if you and Belinda tried together? Andie, as well, if she can boost your abilities.'

It was worth a shot, so the three of us stood in a circle holding hands. I was conscious of Celeste and Ethan standing nearby, adding their support. Angel took control of the link, and I felt the power surging around her, bolstered by Andie's strength. The hairs on my arms rose and a shiver swept over me at how powerful the three of us were combined.

'Think about Lachlan and Dr Frankel, about what they might be doing now,' said Angel.

When I did what she wanted, I felt her form some kind of mental probe with our combined thoughts, sending it outwards. It roamed away from the house, and I could follow it with my mind's eye as it sought the target. It rolled over Easton, but no matter how hard Angel pushed, it didn't find anything.

Eventually the probe dissipated, the strength of our sending depleted.

'It's no use. I can't sense them at all,' said Angel, letting my hand drop, a thread of fear in her mental voice.

The knowledge she was afraid lingered with me. She had been using her psychic abilities all her life. She could throw fireballs, and had done so to free herself and the others less than a month ago.

If she was scared of what might happen next, then I had reason to be terrified.

I had a feeling I had more to worry about than losing my eyes.

13

With nothing else to be done other than wait for Dr Frankel to make his move, Scott and I left. I was sure Mum and Dad would be wondering what was taking us so long. It wasn't until we were halfway there that I remembered Dr Frankel saying something about him having delayed Scott to keep him away from the Vision Centre.

So I asked him about it.

'It was nothing. Don't worry about it.'

The trouble was, the tightness of his voice said it was something. 'You need to tell me what happened, Scott. I need to know.'

He heaved a sigh. 'Fine. I got suspended.'

'What? Why?'

'Detective Johnson found out I was using my leave to protect you and I got ordered to the station to explain myself. He wouldn't listen to a word I said and, as I broke the rules, I was suspended pending an investigation. The Easton Police Department don't hold with their officers getting involved with witnesses and clients.'

While I was angry he had been suspended, his use of the word "involved" made me smile. But then, it wouldn't last surely. 'After what happened today, they will lift the suspension, right? I was attacked, and almost kidnapped for the second time. They have to know now that I need protection.'

'I don't know. I didn't get a chance to talk to the officers who were on scene. So I'm not sure what's going to happen next.'

'What's going to happen is that you get your job back.'

'I hope so, but I get the feeling Detective Johnson doesn't like me very much.'

'It will be fine. I'm sure it will.'

'You see that in a vision?'

I gave a low laugh. 'No. I only seem to see bad stuff happening. But I will make it fine as soon as we get this Dr Frankel arrested and find Lachlan. Not even Detective Johnson can ignore what's been happening then.'

'Yeah, we'll see about that.'

We arrived home and the next hour was spent reassuring Mum and Dad that I was okay. I had a few aches and pains, but was otherwise fine. I took a long hot shower to soak away the aches and emerged feeling much better than before. When I returned to the lounge the house was silent.

'Hello?'

A hand touched my arm.

'Hey there, you look a lot better,' said Scott.

'I feel a lot better.' I let him lead me to the couch and sank onto it. 'Where are Mum and Dad?' The house was silent around us.

'Your dad got a call to come into work just after you hopped into the shower. Apparently it was some kind of emergency and they needed him there straight away. Your mum has ducked next door. Seems the elderly neighbour had a fall and required some assistance. I offered to go, but your mum said Mrs Fitzsimmons needed help of a more personal nature and my presence would not be appreciated.'

'Oh no, I hope Mrs Fitzsimmons is going to be okay.'

'Me too. From what your mum said, she's a real character.'

'That's one way to describe her,' I said, smiling as I

remembered some of the crazy antics Mrs Fitzsimmons had got up to over the years.

My smile vanished as a vision hit.

I stiffened, feeling Scott's arms wrap around me, but I had no time to focus on that. All I could see was a wall of electrical equipment, sparks shooting between them and sending flames spiralling into the air. There were four people in the room, all wearing white lab coats with "Anderson's Industrial" emblazoned below the collar on the left-hand side in red embroidery. They began to cough when gas was emitted from a canister connected to one of the pieces of equipment. The four of them dropped to their hands and knees, in search of breathable air.

It was a lab of some kind, big interior windows showing a group of people standing in a hallway on the other side. Some of them rushed to the door and tugged on it. It wouldn't open. It had a keypad and a slide for a security card.

One of the people on the floor of the lab crawled toward the door, a card gripped in his hands, but he was overcome with a coughing fit and fell two metres away. I heard dull thuds as people on the outside banged heavy items against the windows in a futile effort to break what had to be reinforced glass.

A security guard appeared, running down the outside hall, fumbling with his swipe card as the people watching on urged him to hurry. He dropped the card, picked it up and then swiped it, quickly keying in the code to allow the door to open. Arm up to shield his mouth and nose, he rushed into the room. He stopped to grab the arms of the man closest to the door, dragging him backward, face going red as he held his breath to avoid inhaling whatever it was that had struck the man and the others down.

The guard stumbled out the door, coughing violently. He

handed the man he'd rescued to those waiting and went to re-enter the laboratory. He made it a few metres in before he collapsed near the ominously still body of one of the scientists.

As I watched, the gas began to spill out of the open doorway, winding its way through the air vents as those who had taken charge of the man the guard had rescued started coughing. They stumbled backward, seeking to retreat, but it was too late. The thuds as their bodies hit the ground echoed in my head as the vision released me.

I came to, cradled in Scott's arms.

'There's going to be some kind of toxic gas leak, at Anderson's Industrial.' I filled Scott in on what I'd seen. 'They're all going to die, even the people who try to rescue them. And it's going to get worse. The lockdown procedure failed, so the gas was spreading into the rest of the building. You have to stop it from happening.'

Scott stood and I soon heard him talking to Detective Johnson.

'I'm telling you, it will happen. You need to get someone over there now to clear the place out, before you have a major disaster on your hands.'

After a short and tense conversation, Scott hung up his phone.

'He wouldn't listen. It's as though he didn't even care that people are going to die.'

'He didn't believe you?'

'I think he believed me. All of your visions have come true. It's more like he didn't care.'

'You need to get over there. It felt as if it was going to happen soon. You have to save those people.'

'I am not leaving you alone.'

'Mum's just next door. She'll be back soon. You have to

go now, Scott. I get these visions for a reason. You have to save those people.'

He didn't like it, but I eventually got him to leave. I locked the door behind him, and then sat back on the couch to wait for him to call to say he'd been able to save everyone.

I was sitting there, waiting, when I heard the roller door to the garage go up.

Sure it was Dad returning from work, I didn't think anything of it. I was too worried about Scott. The security guard had been overcome by the gas when he'd entered the lab. What if that happened to Scott as well?

I was nibbling my bottom lip when the door connecting the garage to the house opened up and I heard footsteps coming my way.

'Did you get everything sorted at work, Dad? Scott said there was some kind of emergency.'

'Hello, Belinda. Good to see you weren't hurt by the events of this morning.'

I screamed at the sound of Dr Frankel's voice, standing and trying to back away to the front door, to get out of there.

'Now, now, there's no need for that.'

Someone grabbed me from behind and a cloth was shoved in front of my face. It stank, and I fought not to breathe whatever was on it, struggling against the arms that were holding me, but I couldn't break free.

Soon I had to breathe, inhaling whatever was on the cloth, growing increasingly dizzy.

My struggles ceased, head flopping to the side as I felt myself being picked up.

The last thing I heard was Lachlan's voice as he told Dr Frankel to open the boot.

I woke to a loud bang, sitting up, struggling to make sense of what had happened.

The vision. Scott leaving. Dr Frankel appearing in my house and whisking me away.

I shuddered, hands going to my face. Had he finished what he'd started that morning? Had he taken my eyes?

I sagged back in relief at finding my eyes were still intact.

'Don't get too comfortable. I'm not sure how long I can get him to hold off on the surgery.'

I stiffened, recognising Lachlan's voice.

'You stopped him. Why?'

'Don't get me wrong, I didn't do it to help you. I'm not suddenly morphing into the good guy here.'

There was an edge to his words, a hint of desperation, as if what he was saying and what he was thinking were two different things.

'How do you do it?' Lachlan asked. 'How do you stop the pain?'

I shook my head. 'What do you mean?'

'The pain from the visions. How do you block it? I've watched you when you were having a vision. You're not in pain. How?'

'I don't understand. Do you feel pain when you have a vision?'

'It's excruciating. Like someone is ripping my brain to shreds. He gives me mediation to dull the pain, but it's never enough. I need to know what you use.'

'I don't use anything. I've never had pain with one of my visions.' Not physical pain anyway.

'You're lying. It always hurts. Dr Frankel said it's the price we pay for having a gift. You need to tell me how you stop it.'

Before I could answer, convince him I was telling the truth, a door opened somewhere nearby.

'Too late,' said Lachlan, pushing me down and winding a

thick strap over me, pinning me to the bed. 'He's here, and you're going to lose your eyes. I could have stopped him, if you'd been straight with me. Now it's your turn to feel the pain.'

'Wait, no,' I said, hearing him walk away. 'Please don't leave me. I'll find a way to help you, I promise.'

I would help him, take him to Angel and the others. Surely between us we could sort out why the visions were causing him pain and fix it. Ethan hadn't been able to restore my sight, but maybe this was something he could heal.

But Lachlan was right, there was no time.

'Good to see you're finally awake, Belinda. I was starting to think I'd used too much chloroform to subdue you.'

'Why are you doing this? What do you want with me?'

'Having someone who can predict the future is a highly desirable skill to certain customers of mine. If I can deliver a functioning psychic, it will enable them to get ahead of competitors and the authorities.'

'You have Lachlan. Why do you need two of us?'

'Unfortunately, Lachlan's track record with accuracy has taken a downslide lately. I need someone with a proven track record, and from what I have observed your visions are eerily accurate. Lachlan often only sees what might happen, not what will happen. Although he does have the advantage of being able to make people see things that are not there.'

He gave a low chuckle. 'As you no doubt discovered when he sent you a vision of a toxic gas accident in a laboratory all the way on the other side of town.'

I sucked in a breath. The vision had been fake, a way to get me alone.

While I felt relief to know Scott was not heading into a dangerous situation, the knowledge this would get him in even more trouble with his superiors made me angry.

'You have no right to play with people's lives, or their minds. I will never do what you want. Never.'

'You will do what I say, when I say. By the time I hand you over to my customer, you will be as docile as a lamb and obey any command. But I'm afraid you won't like the conditioning that will be necessary before that handover can take place. I need to break you, the way I did Lachlan. Step one will be to remove your eyes.'

I felt him place his hands on my head, holding it still as he tried to clamp it in place with a strap. I fought against him, hating the lethargy sweeping through my body.

'This is going to hurt, but in the end you will thank me. The medication I've started you on has many benefits, one of which is addiction.'

Addiction. Was that what was causing Lachlan so much pain, withdrawal symptoms?

I struggled even harder, striving to call out with my mental voice. Angel had been able to connect with me, earlier that day. Surely I could do the same.

I called out to her in my head, but all I felt was an echo as my shout reverberated in the air around me.

It was no use. Whatever ability I had, long distance telepathy was not part of it.

Lachlan was close by.

Could I get him to help me?

'Lachlan!' I called out to him with all my strength, blocking out the feel of the clamps Dr Frankel was attaching to my eyes to keep them open.

A sharp sting under my left eye made me cry out and I doubled the strength of my call with the pain as booster.

But Lachlan either didn't hear me or didn't care.

I had to get out of there.

But how?

14

Instead of calling out to Lachlan, I focused on Dr Frankel. He'd said Lachlan could send me visions, make me see things that weren't there. Could I do the same to Dr Frankel?

Sucking up my courage, I fought to get through to Dr Frankel's mind. I could feel him hovering over me, feel his anticipation as he prepared to make the first cut. I could see myself, face scrunched up in fear on the operating table. I was looking through his eyes. I latched on to that thought, forcing an image of him letting me go to replace the one of him cutting into my eye.

He winced, giving a mental shrug as he tried to dislodge me from his mind, but I latched on even tighter, determined to make him see what I wanted.

I formed the scenario one image at a time, showing him releasing the straps holding me down and then stepping away. I repeated the images over and over again, not letting him have any respite.

He stumbled backward, hands dropping from my head.

A moment later I felt his hands working on the straps, and they loosened around me. I shoved them off and slid my legs over the side of the cool metal table. Dr Frankel shuffled backward, and then stopped at my silent command.

Both horrified and exhilarated with the knowledge I could control him, I got him to lead me to the door. As before, I could see through his eyes. We were in a long hallway with fluorescent lights hanging from the ceiling. The walls, floor, everything I could see was a faded grey, old and encrusted with dirt. There were no windows, only doors, and no indication what way I should go.

Focusing my thoughts on escape, I gave Dr Frankel a mental prod, holding his arm as he started walking. We went through several doors, down two flights of stairs, and through another door before we finally reached an exterior door.

It was late afternoon, shadows rolling in, as I scanned my surroundings to get an idea of where I was and what to do next. We must have come out at the back of a large building. All I could see was an empty loading bay bordered by dense woods. There was no traffic noise, nothing to tell me where we were. I got Dr Frankel to turn in a circle, using his eyes to see, hoping something would appear to help me.

Panic washed over me when there was nothing and my control over Dr Frankel wavered. He groaned, hands going to his head before he collapsed to the ground, senseless.

The second he lost consciousness I lost the advantage of seeing through his eyes.

What was I supposed to do now?

Once more, I tried to reach Angel but it was no use.

How long did I have before Dr Frankel regained consciousness and had a third attempt at taking my eyes?

Forcing myself to think, to not panic, I started walking across the loading bay toward the woods, hoping I was going in the right direction. If I could get to the trees, hide myself amongst them, maybe I could wait it out until I was rescued. Angel had sent Scott to my rescue last time. He could be on his way now. I just had to find a safe place to wait for him.

I pushed aside the thought that last time Angel had contacted me telepathically to tell me I was in danger and that help was on the way.

I had to believe I was not on my own.

Hands out in front of me, I walked slowly, feeling the

change in the ground beneath my feet as I stepped off the concrete at the edge of the loading bay. My fingers brushed against the bark of a tree and I wound my way past it, arms outstretched in search of the next one.

When I finally felt a mental pulse I almost cried out in relief.

Then I stiffened. It didn't feel like Angel.

'If you ever want to see your cop boyfriend again, you will do exactly what I say.'

'Lachlan?'

Brow creased, I spun in a slow circle, trying to sense his presence. As far as I could tell no one was nearby.

An image popped into my head. Scott, eyes closed, down on the ground, blood trickling from a gash on his left temple. He was in a small clearing, surrounded by tees that looked similar to what I had seen when I'd used Dr Frankel's eyes. It had to be nearby, and I turned my head, trying to see if I could hear anything to pinpoint his location.

As I watched on, helpless, Scott opened his eyes.

'Don't listen to him, Belinda. Stay away.'

A boot appeared, kicking Scott in the side. He groaned, pain contorting his features as he clutched his side.

'You want your boyfriend back in one piece, you need to get moving. Dr Frankel will be waking up real soon, and then your last chance to save lover boy will be gone, along with your eyes.'

My view of Scott disappeared, leaving me in darkness once more.

With Lachlan's ability to plant visions in my head, I couldn't trust that what he had shown me was real. He wouldn't have had time to kidnap Scott after leaving me with Dr Frankel, but what if he'd done it while I was unconscious and before I'd woken up? I should have got Dr Frankel to give me his phone, to call for help. Now I was in the middle of nowhere, with no way of contacting anyone. But I couldn't take the risk of not doing what Lachlan wanted, for Scott's sake, in case this was not a trick.

'Don't hurt him. I'll do whatever you want, but you will need to come and get me,' I said, buying myself time to think.

'Not happening.'

'I'm blind. How am I supposed to come to you if I can't see where I'm going?'

A new vision filled my head, but this time it was different. It was as if I could see again, Lachlan using his ability to show me where I was. I turned my head and saw the building I had escaped from through the trees, Dr Frankel's body still slumped on the ground near the door where we'd exited.

I looked deeper into the woods, head reeling as a split second delay in the visual feed blinded me. When I could see again, an image of me in the white gown from my nightmares appeared in front of me. The vision me turned, expression blank, and then set off through the trees.

With the image of myself as a guide, I followed as best I could.

With the delay in what Lachlan saw through my eyes being translated back to me, it was slow going. I kept a hand up near my face to shield me from stray branches. The vision I followed was imperfect and I had to take care placing my feet in case I tripped on something.

It was eerie, to follow my own image, with someone else controlling my sight.

How was it that I could see while Lachlan used my eyes, and yet I saw nothing?

Up ahead, the vision of me pushed past a low bush and then vanished.

I hurried to the spot where I'd seen her, me, last, and stepped into the clearing from my original vision.

Scott was on the ground, the dirt and leaves clinging to the blood smeared on the side of his face.

His image flickered and disappeared.

My borrowed sight vanished, leaving me blind once more.

Footsteps sounded behind me, and a hand gripped my arm.

I pulled away, but he held tightly, wrenching me up against his chest.

'Tell me how to stop the pain.'

'Where's Scott?'

'No idea. I just used his image to get you to come to me.'

Relief surged through me. Scott was okay. Lachlan didn't have him.

He gave me a shake.

'I'll hunt him down and hurt him for real if you don't start talking.'

Chilling though his words were, it was the desperation in his voice that got to me the most. 'Lachlan, I already told you I don't get pain with my visions. But I want to help you.'

'No you don't. You're just like Frankel. You want to use me. You think I'll help you escape, take you back to your boyfriend, if you act all nice.'

He was right, I did want him to help me, but that wasn't the only reason I'd let him lead me further into the woods. 'I'm nothing like Dr Frankel. What he's done to you is wrong. He needs to be stopped. Come with me. My friends and I will find a way to stop the pain.'

'How?'

'I don't know yet, but we'll figure it out together. Angel and the others can do amazing things. I'm sure they can help you.'

219

I thought better about mentioning that Ethan could heal, not sure if his ability worked on someone suffering from addiction. That is, if I was right about how Dr Frankel was controlling Lachlan.

A shudder went through his body, his grip on my arm tightening.

'You don't know what it's like. The things he makes me do. He'll do the same to you, once he takes your eyes. You'll never be free.'

I swallowed down the horror of his words. 'Together we can stop him. All of us.'

For a moment his grip faltered, but then he wrenched me around so I was facing him. 'You need to tell me how to stop the pain now. The medication isn't helping anymore. It's making it worse.'

'Lachlan. What are you doing?'

We both spun around at Dr Frankel's shout. I couldn't see him, but there was no mistaking the suspicion in his voice.

'Bring her back to the lab, now, so I can finish the procedure.'

Lachlan gripped my arm. 'I can't do that. She's coming with me. She's going to fix me.'

Relief flooded me at his words. I'd got through to him. He was going to let me help him.

'Don't be ridiculous. You know I'm the only one who can help you. Bring her here, and I'll make sure you get an extra dose of your medication.'

'I don't want an extra dose. I just want the pain to stop.'

'And I can help you with that.'

'No you can't. You don't want to help me. You just want to use me. Same as you want to use Belinda. But I'm done being your patsy. I'm done making people see things that aren't there so you can get your way. I'm done hurting people on your say so. It's over. I don't work for you anymore. We're leaving, and don't try to stop us.'

'Don't be a fool, Lachlan. You are nothing without me. I got you off the streets, I fed and clothed you, gave your life purpose, when no one else wanted anything to do with you. To everyone else you are a freak of nature, an aberration. But to me you are precious, as is Belinda. Now that I have the two of you I will be able to expand my program, command even higher prices for those seeking to use your abilities. You will be able to live like a king, we both will, on the money we can make using Belinda's ability to see the future. Don't throw that all away for a lie. She doesn't want to help you. She'll say whatever it is she thinks you want her to say, just to get you to side with her.'

'You know that's not true,' I said to Lachlan, keeping my voice low. 'You can sense how much I want to help you, just as I can sense how hurt and confused you are.' I opened up to him, letting him see my determination to help him and the compassion I felt, holding nothing back. 'Don't listen to Dr Frankel. Together we will find a way to stop the pain.'

Lachlan tugged me closer, allowing me to see through his eyes as he faced Dr Frankel, shadows making a sinister rendition of his face.

I heard a noise behind us, but with Lachlan's attention focused on the doctor, when I turned around all I could see was what he saw.

Too late, the flicker of Dr Frankel's eyes as he looked behind us gave a warning.

There came a thud, and then Lachlan groaned, letting go of me and slumping to the ground.

'Run, Belinda,' he said in my head, sending me a vision of the way through the woods.

'No, I won't leave you,' I said, crouching and feeling for

his prone body.

Arms grabbed me, roughly pulling me back, and I fought against them. Then whoever had hold of me gave a cry and let go.

'I don't know how long I can hold them. You need to go and get help,' said Lachlan, strain evident in his mental voice.

I gasped, realising he was using his abilities to confuse Dr Frankel and his accomplice.

I felt an urge to run, and even as I realised it came from him, I couldn't block out the need to obey. I set off at a run, dress tangling in the branches as I made my way through the woods. Time came to a standstill as Lachlan overrode my own instinct and got me moving.

I came to a road and flagged down a passing car, begging the driver to call the police.

Once that was done I wanted to go back to Lachlan, but my vision cut off, leaving me blind. I could do nothing but wait for the police to arrive, knowing they would be too late.

Hours later Scott wrapped me in his arms and tried to console me when another officer said the searchers had found no sign of either Lachlan or Dr Frankel.

They were gone, with no indication of where they had fled to or if Lachlan was okay. He'd saved me, sacrificed himself so I could get help. But it had come too late for him.

'Hey,' said Scott, hugging me against him. 'It will be okay. The entire police force is on the lookout for him and that crazy doctor. They'll find them.'

Considering they'd been looking for Dr Frankel for a month with no success, I didn't hold much faith in that. It would be up to me and Angel, and the others, to find Lachlan and free him from Dr Frankel's clutches.

Scott gave me another hug. 'I do have some good news, though. With everything that happened today, my suspension was lifted. I've even been asked to join a new taskforce that deals with incidents of a more specialised nature.'

'Specialised? As in visions?'

'Yep. With all the weird occurrences taking place in Easton over the last year and a half, they've decided they need a team dedicated to investigating the strange cases. It's headed up by a former homicide detective, Sam Lockwood, and also has civilians delivering expert advice. I've been asked to invite you to become part of the team, with me acting as your liaison.'

'Really?' A kernel of excitement slowly built in my stomach at the thought of working closely with Scott. 'How does Detective Johnson feel about that?'

'Don't know and I don't care. He's not part of the team. In fact, he's under investigation for the way he handled your case. Seems I'm not the only one to think he was deliberately mishandling things. So, what do you say? Want to help me fight crime?'

'Yeah, I do.' Maybe Angel and the others could be part of the taskforce too. A group of people dedicated to using their abilities to help others. I liked the sound of that.

15

With Dad holding one of my hands, and Mum holding the other, I gave a nod. 'I'm ready,' I said.

'Okay, then, let's do this,' said Dr Randle.

A moment later cool fingers brushed against my face, skin pulling as she tugged at the tape holding the bandage covering my left eye secure.

Air brushed against the exposed flesh when she pulled the bandage off, but I kept my eyes closed as she repeated the process with the right eye.

'You can open your eyes now, Belinda,' said Dr Randle.

Sucking in a breath, feeling Dad give my hand a reassuring squeeze, I slowly opened my eyes.

Tears spilled down my cheeks, and I shook my head.

'Belinda, honey, it's okay,' said Mum. 'We'll find another way to get your sight back.'

Her voice was thick with unshed tears and I turned to her and smiled, shaking my head. 'I'm not crying because I'm blind. I'm crying because I'm happy,' I said to the blur that was her face.

As I blinked away tears, the blur sharpened until I could see her familiar features. 'Hey, there,' I said. 'Long time no see.'

Then I turned to Dad and smiled into his brown eyes.

Seconds later I was engulfed in his arms, Dad making no effort to hide his tears. A long time later, he pulled away and waited patiently with Mum as Dr Randle checked over my eyes.

'It all looks good. The incisions are closing over and there is no sign your eyes are rejecting the new tissue. They'll feel gritty for a while as they adjust, so you need to resist the urge to rub them, especially in your sleep.'

She showed me the hard, plastic eye patches she wanted me to wear at night for the next two weeks.

'You also need to keep them closed as much as possible for the next forty-eight hours as the healing continues. But other than that, you are good to go. My receptionist has the scripts for the eye drops you will need to use and I will see you back here for a check up in one month's time. Of course, if you have any problems don't hesitate to call.'

Dad helped me off the examination chair while Mum grabbed her handbag. His grip on my elbow was light as he directed me toward the door.

I stopped and placed my hand over his, gently removing it. 'It's okay, Dad. You don't need to show me the way anymore.'

Fresh tears welled in his eyes as he gave a nod. Then he leaned in for another hug. 'I'm so proud of you.'

He released me and stepped back, allowing me to be the one to open the door.

I stepped through, immediately scanning the waiting room for Scott.

I'd seen him in the visions Lachlan had sent me, but this would be the first time I got to see him with my own eyes.

He stood up, banging into the coffee table in his haste to greet me, his blue eyes roaming my face, uncertainty in their depths.

I gave him a smile, taking in the wavy brown hair that looked as though he'd been running his hands through it numerous times. My fingers itched to smooth it down. But for some reason, I couldn't move.

Half aware of Mum and Dad moving over to the front counter, I stared at Scott.

He was so tall. I'd known it on some level, but to see him now, how handsome and strong he looked, it took my breath away.

He sidestepped the coffee table and came over to me, one hand coming up to brush my cheek, smoothing the skin irritated by the tape.

'It worked,' he said. 'You can see again.'

I gave a nod, not trusting my voice with him standing so close, his fingers now caressing my cheek.

His smile widened and he flung his arms around me, lifting me up and spinning me in a circle.

I laughed, breathless, and was still laughing when he set me back on my feet. Then he cupped my face in his hands, leaning forward to press his lips against mine.

I fell into the kiss, marvelling at the taste and feel of him.

A loud cough brought me back to reality as Scott's arms snaked around me.

I turned and smiled at Dad.

'Ready to go home?' Dad asked.

I didn't need to look at Scott to answer for both of us. 'I'll be there soon. There's somewhere Scott and I have to go first.'

Minutes later Scott and I pulled up outside Angel's house. She and the others were all waiting inside, ready to celebrate the miracle that was my restored eyesight.

But as much as I was looking forward to celebrating with my new friends, there was something else I needed to take care of first.

I closed my eyes and reached out with my senses, searching nearby for the sparks I associated with the occupants of the house.

There, the flash of light that was Celeste, the rumble of earth for Ethan, and the fire that burned at Angel's core. I could even pick up Andie, the reservoir of strength residing deep within her. I pushed my senses further, but was unable to find the quicksilver image that indicated Lachlan.

With a sigh, I opened my eyes and turned to Scott.

'Still no sign of him?'

His voice was neutral, but I knew he was torn about my desire to find Lachlan.

I shook my head. 'We have to find him. He needs our help. Dr Frankel is abusing his ability. I wouldn't be here now if it wasn't for what he did. I owe him.'

Scott reached out and took my hand.

'We'll find him, I promise.'

Hand in hand, we walked to the front door to where Angel waited to let us in. As I took my first real look at the new friends I'd made, I knew Scott was right. With this lot on my side, anything was possible.

ACKNOWLEDGEMENTS

It's that time again when I get to thank the people who have helped me on my writing journey. I am lucky to have so many who support me, both family, friends and readers. Without them this book would not be possible. They are there cheering me on every step of the way and I am so grateful to them all.

Special thanks to my mum for being my first fan, and for loving everything I write, and for my hubby and kids who don't complain too much when I disappear into my writing cave. Donna, Jennifer and Jael are constant supporters, there when I need to brainstorm and bounce ideas off. They're also always the first to demand their copies when the print books arrive.

Huge thanks to Mariah Sinclair for creating yet another amazing cover, it is so very very pretty, and to Sally Odgers for her editing expertise which helped make my story the best it could be. I also want to give a special shout out to my amazing beta readers, Sue-Ellen Pashley, Danni Line, Linda Higgins, Cass Fowler and Nikki Banks. You ladies ROCK!

Finally, thanks to the readers who gave Arcane Awakenings a chance. I hope you will stick with me to find out what happens next.

ABOUT THE AUTHOR

Shelley Russell Nolan is an avid reader who began writing her own stories at sixteen. Her first completed manuscript featured brain eating aliens and a butt kicking teenage heroine. Since then she has spent her time creating fantasy worlds where death is only the beginning and even freaks can fall in love.

The first two books in her debut adult urban fantasy series, *Lost Reaper* and *Winged Reaper*, were published by Atlas Productions in 2016, with *Silver Reaper* published in 2017 to complete the series. Odyssey Books will be publishing the first book in a new post-apocalyptic series in September 2018.

Born in New Zealand, moving to Australia with her family when she was seven, Shelley currently lives in Central Queensland, Australia, with her husband and two young children. They share their home with two wrecking ball kitties, a deformed budgerigar, and one pipsqueak of a dog that is fairly normal as dogs go.

Shelley loves to hear from her readers so feel free to contact her on Facebook or leave a review on Amazon or Goodreads or on her website - shelleyrussellnolan.com

ALSO BY SHELLEY RUSSELL NOLAN

Arcane Awakenings Books One and Two

A hidden past. An uncertain future.

In *Angel Fire*, all Andie wants is acceptance, a task made difficult thanks to the nightmare that's plagued her for the past fifteen years. Then she learns it's a terrifying memory of the night she lost her identical twin. When Angel's spirit calls to her, begging to be saved, Andie is determined to discover what really happened the night her sister died.

The story continues in *Wild Lightning*, when Celeste wakes in a mental institution with no memory of who she is or why she can shoot lightning from her fingertips. Spurred on by a vision of Angel, Celeste escapes and searches for answers as her captors close in.

Andie and Celeste must battle ruthless adversaries as they seek to uncover the truth, but will this lead to a future more dangerous than what they've left behind?

Arcane Awakenings – a fast-paced paranormal fantasy novella series.

Lost Reaper
(Book One of the Reaper Series)

The first dead body I ever saw was my own.

For twenty-five year old Tyler Morgan, being murdered was easy. Easy in comparison with working for the Grim Reaper.

Jonathon Grimm may have brought her back from the dead in exchange for working as a reaper for her hometown, Easton, but she has to find his lost reaper before she can enjoy her second chance at life. Only ... the lost reaper isn't actually lost. He has a new body and a new life and no intention of turning himself in, even if it means giving Tyler her life back.

Tyler begins the grisly task of reaping the souls of Easton's dead while searching for the reaper. He could be anyone – the intriguing detective, Sam Lockwood; the handsome, wealthy Chris Bradbury; or the serial killer stalking the women of Easton. Women who bear an uncanny resemblance to Tyler.

But what is the ancient secret, hidden from mankind, that has motivated Grimm to choose Tyler for the morbid task?

As the killer closes in and Grimm's deadline draws closer, Tyler discovers she is fighting a much bigger threat than the Grim Reaper and time is running out for everyone.

Winged Reaper
(Book Two of the Reaper Series)

Secrets, lies and the Grim Reaper: a recipe for disaster!

Twenty-five-year-old Tyler Morgan is only alive--technically reborn--because the Grim Reaper offered her a job. Now she has to find a way to stop her 'boss' from starting a war that threatens the survival of mankind.

Weak and in need of fresh souls, the Grim Reaper has sent his Wraiths to Tyler's hometown, Easton, and by the time he gets his fill, it could turn into a graveyard.

Tyler's resolve is tested when old secrets surface and a new betrayal has her questioning where her loyalties lie.

Supported by the intriguing detective, Sam Lockwood; the handsome, wealthy Chris Bradbury; and sources she never expected to come to her aid, Tyler must fight her way to the truth if she is ever to find the strength to harness the powers she has inherited, and vanquish the Grim Reaper forever.

Silver Reaper
(Book Three of the Reaper Series)

How far would you go to save those marked for Death?

When the call to reap uncovers a new threat to Easton and its inhabitants, Tyler is drawn back into a world she thought she'd left behind.

Forced to face her greatest fears, she seeks to uncover the identity of the rogue reaper murdering men employed by her former ally. But the search leads her to a conspiracy decades in the making.

With the line between friends and enemies blurring, Tyler begins to question her loyalties as she fights to stop the storm threatening to engulf Easton. But when the Grim Reaper offers the last hope, death might be the least of her problems.

Who can Tyler trust when even her allies want her dead?